CONTEMPT

OF

CONGRESS

CONTEMPT
OF
CONGRESS

BABY BOOMERS TALK
SEX, RACE, POLITICS,
ENVIRONMENT & REVOLUTION

by

Barry Leonardini

FRESH CLEAN DAY PUBLISHING
Woodside, California

ISBN 13: 978-0-9728416-3-4

ISBN 10: 0-9728416-3-6

Library of Congress Control Number: 2010920035

MANUFACTURED IN THE UNITED STATES OF AMERICA

FRESH CLEAN DAY PUBLISHING

Woodside, California

www.freshcleanday.com

barry@freshcleanday.com

Phil Di Caesari and his long time friend Gene Ray were having their regular lunch. Mostly it was just the two of them now. Many of their mutual friends had passed away. Both were 60 something baby boomers who were taught at the Saint Ignatius College Preparatory and the University of San Francisco which were both run by the Jesuits. The Jesuits taught well. And if the students were not paying attention then maybe a swift slap might startle them. The best curriculum is the one that helps the pupil locate which phase of repeating history one was currently in. Jesuits avoid political correct history. They want their students to have a needle on their compass.

Phil was an honor student who went on to Wall Street and did very well. He rode horses for many years but lost his last in 2005. Now he fenced competitively. He was divorced with one child. But he still had a warm and close relationship with his former wife. He was a man of passion who generated compelling concepts. Gene was also an honor student. He became an attorney. He was quite brilliant and had a natural ability for calling things by their right name. He wasn't thrown off by descriptions or names that were not accurate or meant to deceive. He was married with two children. He was a dispassionate man who needed a logical argument to be moved. After practicing law for so many years he reserved judgment on any issue. It was a survival exercise. An attorney never knows which side of an argument he will be called to plead. Lawyers learn to live and thrive in the moral ambivalence zone. Agreement and disagreement were possible on various subjects when Phil and Gene conversed. Minds could be changed if an argument was persuasive. Consequently there was never wasted effort.

The 2-3 hour lunch was at Sam's Grill and Seafood Restaurant in San Francisco. It had been in existence for over one hundred years. The secret to their success was a simple menu using quality ingredients that were well prepared and served professionally. It is remarkable that all the owners had followed the original philosophy passed on in oral history. The ambiance included classic dark wood paneled walls and private booths. There was an attractive, extensive collection of early twentieth century wild fowl prints hanging on the walls. All this and the tasty and potent cocktails gave the feeling to patrons that they could be in any sophisticated city in the world. The setting was apolitical. But it was a popular place for multi-spectrum political discussions. The flying and pumping elbows were in the act of eating and drinking as well as dramatizing political view points. There was always the sound of conversation which had a sustaining energy.

Phil and Gene were perusing the menu without seriously considering ordering much differently than they had before.

Phil mutters, "I will have a half dozen fresh oysters and the Rex Sole and a side of creamed spinach."

Gene, without looking up from the menu, says "I'll have the Sand Dabs, the oysters and the creamed spinach also. Gene, do you want a cocktail or wine?"

Phil with an inspiration adds, "Oysters, I lick 'em and warm 'em. They seem to spring alive on my tongue."

Amused Gene picks up his head and looks at Phil with the begged straight line, "What do your dates think about the double *entendre* gambit?"

"Well, no one ever leaves. You know they're always looking and listening for clues. The gals try so hard and ask for so little. I'm going to have a Negroni. Want one?" replied Phil who's feeling satisfied with his pre-lunch entertainment.

"Yes. A Negroni sounds great. Phil remember you're a white male. When you use words like 'clues' in front of people you don't know in San Francisco, you risk being thought a bigot for even obliquely acknowledging critical thinking or personal taste?" Gene commented in a voice and demeanor of a traffic cop who is telling a driver to watch out or next time he will get a ticket. Gene continued, "How's the fencing going in those national competitions?"

"Where have you been Gene? White males are a minority in the state and I think a minority in the city. I'm going to use my minority status for activism. When you are a majority race then opinions are bigoted. But when you're a minority race, then opinions are righteous activism. Fencing? I've found I can lose in Atlanta and Chicago just like I lose in the Bay Area." Phil said in a self mocking way. "But the exposure has helped me when I come home. There's nothing more instructive than losing to top rated fencers but knowing how you lost and adjusting. There's an old Russian fencing master saying, ' There are two types of fencers that you will face in the future. One type is a better fencer than you. The other type is just dangerous'. The moral? Don't ever relax. I tried to get over to Oakland last night for one of my regular fencing workouts and I had to turn back. Traffic heading towards the bridge was backed up for a mile. The point and click commuter drivers were fuming."

Lunch came and the drinks came regularly. The food was prepared for the eye and the tongue. The oysters came first. Six clean sparklers laying in their half shell on a bed of ice in an oblong platter. The Rex Sole and the Sand Dabs was filleted into small strips. They were laid across and filled a large plate. The fish platter included a couple of small boiled potatoes which were lightly sprinkled with parsley. The very tasty *ala carte* creamed spinach came in a small bowl. It was highly seasoned yet did not overwhelm. The Negronis were served up and made with vodka and both types of vermouth but without the sparkling water. The original 1920's Negroni — divined by an Italian count of the same name — was made with gin, Compari and only dry vermouth with a sparkling water floater.

"Summer is here. Baseball and women fashions are some of the seasonal entertainment." said Phil coming up for air after somewhat wolfing small bits of all his plates. "The hemlines go up and the necklines come down and cleavages appear with the rest of the strike zone outlined and beckoning. Look at the lovely that is coming in. The thighs, breasts ... the words are almost onomatopoeic. The speakers of the Indo-European language still get their message across even with thousands of years of language corruption." Phil thought how little basic difference there is in a routine lunch for him and a patrician of Rome some 2000 years ago. Food, spirits, girl watching, sport references and political conversation which was due any minute now.

And along comes Gene right on time. He pitches one, "Good bye to our Republic. Like Rome, it has predictably defaulted into an old fashion mob-ruled democracy which also nailed the Athenians. The roots of our demise are in Maryland circa 1810. It's not going to be pretty."

"Isn't that the state that Madame Speaker Guida Fascista-Cana comes from?" asks Phil, self satisfied that he pointed out that connection.

"The same. There must be something in the Maryland water. The roots of our problem with democracy is Maryland started white male suffrage in 1810. Other states quickly followed. Suffrage separated the requirement to own property before one could vote. When that connection is gone then anything can happen in government." said Gene with a dismal conviction and a dread of how long it would take here in the U.S. before a complete breakdown in society.

"You mean white men prone to inaction grouped with other white men without property to push for voting rights without the property requirement? Well it's easier than working for a piece of property. I'm shocked." said a sarcastic, theatrical Phil. But he too dreaded what were the dire possibilities in the future.

Gene adds analytically, "Kind of like primates in the wild do. Mostly they sleep or at rest. Nothing wrong with that. But we advanced primates come up with an excuse for inaction that becomes a cause celebre. For instance, 'We won't work hard because we can't vote'. And then they carry signs and congregate. All that work. But carefully not as much work as necessary to become a property owner. They do the time and motion studies quicker than Einstein's thought experiments. It's definitely a short cut to more wealth and leisure. The ability to short cut is a distinguishing characteristic of homo sapiens. Whether it be with technology to minimize effort or with lies purposeful or not that make it easier for personal advancement. That's why we are such a high maintenance species. Every short cut must be made up by something or someone else. Because we're on a zero sum planet."

Phil continues in a convinced voice, "That poor decision cracked the door open for people like Amos Yomama to become peers. Look at this guy. A crypto, commie from Chicago's dirty, political machine. He's also surrounded by thieving Zionists. Boy are we a long way from our founding principles. Where can I buy a Confederate flag?"

"Who's his agent?" cracks Gene in a higher pitched voice. Gene continues with an instructional tone, "Don't forget Phil, it was 'white male suffrage' before it was woman's suffrage and before black suffrage. All those white guys were and are held captive by their own stupidity. They don't know what's going wrong. The problem is that they are too close to the problem. i.e. the problem is them! They started the disconnect. So you really can't blame others for copying to the point of caricature what lazy white guys have already done. Namely, wanting something for nothing. We witnessed a generational low point with the election of a bona fide moron, white, male, Walker Shrub and his evil Veep, Snarl Chainsaw to the highest offices in the land. That set up a challenge to the left to elect their own caricatures as executives. And so it has come to pass. Voila. The articulate faux sage, communist, black, male, Yomama was elected. It is yet to be determined whether the financial damage that Obama will do will be worse than the criminal war making damage that Shrub did. They both act like retarded individuals because of their one-sided approaches to politics and life."

Phil smiles and nods his understanding and continues, "You're right about the moron. Getting back to Yomama, his lobbyists are his agents just like the same lobbyists were agents for Shrub. The only difference is one lobby group waxes as the other wanes. But it's still money that carries the election. And then there is our peerless Madame Speaker of the House, Guida Fascista-Cana. She is a Snarling Garlic Italian. Oh, the righteous, pandering greed in such grand Kabuki fashion. It's vomit-point politics. Just a few years ago these people would have been thought radicals and many would have liked to have seen them deported. But the relentless drip, drip of political correctness has grown into rogue rapids of new explanations and solutions that have drowned traditional mainstream thinking. And its all courtesy of the alchemy of money together with presumptuous social laws. They'll bankrupt the country with entitlements like YoMamaCare. It includes entitlements to illegals that arrived while we slept. My objections are not about the race factor. It's about having skin in the game. No matter the color of the skin. People must put something in before they get something out."

Gene challenges Phil to be more succinct. Gene is a part-time teacher at the law school at University of California at Berkeley. He can't help but carry over his professor's critical and instructional attitude with his friend," Give me your elevator ride pitch why YoMamaCare is not appropriate. Phil, try to use less words but still inform accurately."

"How many floors Gene?" Phil has been through this drill before. Actually he likes the challenge and sees the merit in the exercise. He continues, "The exploding population argues for smarter coverage. The medical treatment of patients includes almost as much legal, boiler plate, defensive treatment as it does the more important and necessary prudent medical testing. Consequently the costs are driven unnecessarily higher by the attorneys. Add in the astronomical judgments and that's why medical malpractice insurance is so high. There should be a loser pays provision in our legal system to slow down predatory law suits. Also I have an idea on how to control judgment expenses. It would be to stretch out the payments of any judgment over a period of years, rather than to lump-sum someone and their attorney. Are we all in this together or are some just ducks, some just decoys and only the lawyers are the real hunters and gathers? The administration is setting up a generational conflict in their search to find money for the uninsured and the uninvited. The new entitlement legislation reads like an appliance manual. The final stages of any democracy throughout history comes when demands for more benefits meet two realities. One reality is a scarce planet resource fails to satisfy the appetite of an irresponsible civilization. Therefore the civilization collapses. And the other reality is when near broke taxpayers who can't afford any more taxes take their grievances to the streets in revolt. We are not all equal. We are known by our differences. We have a language that can describe and create almost any concept. But that doesn't mean it actually changes real world metaphysics. Ignoring natures laws have wrecked boats, crashed planes and ruined civilizations. Language, concepts or laws that don't honor real time metaphysics will fail to the extent of the deviation."

"That 'ignoring metaphysics' line could be a Nobel Prize winner in the economic category." said a serious Gene. He liked an argument that were short and rock solid.

"Thanks Gene. That's the nicest compliment I've ever received." Said Phil in somewhat of a unbelieving way.

Gene's professor's role showed itself again. He still wasn't satisfied with Phil explanation. He said, "You could have said it in far less words. Remember Phil, use less words and more people will listen and understand. For example, all you had to point out was this, ' YoMamaCare is a de facto huge tax increase that is being sold by the politicians as health care reform. No government should raise taxes on a fragile economy.' That's it. That's all you would have had to say. Then you could fill in a more detailed explanation if people looked like they needed help understanding. You could then add,' This is how it will work like a tax increase. All those newly covered people will be largely paid for by increased insurance premiums across the board on everyone else including small business'. Other revenue will come from new fees or taxes levied on medical device makers which in turn will result in layoffs and less research and development. New taxes will be levied on up- scale insurance coverage. People will be laid off from jobs because of the extra business expense of covering them at work. That will be a self defeating cycle. The net result will be less consumer spending in our 70% consumer economy. This will only accelerate more layoffs etc. which will make it harder for people to pay their insurance premiums etc, etc.'. We're dealing with ideologues coupled with the powerful medical industry lobby interests. That's potent and could be lethal and maybe terminate our economy. But the lobbyists and the politicians will still have their jobs. Also those uninsured 30-40 million that will now be insured are not like you and me who are in good health. These people are ones who couldn't get coverage or don't want coverage. They include some high maintenance types that are suffering from the complications of HIV/AIDS. Theses people only get more expensive to care for over time." instructs a visibly upset Gene.

"Well put Gene. What a mess. The politicians and lobbyists will still have their jobs. Doesn't that frost you? Something has to be done." responds Phil who has been agitated by Gene's scenario. And an agitated Phil never rests until he has a plan of attack or defense.

Gene changes the subject. He's learned that Phil is the most enjoyable when Phil gives extemporaneous opinions on a variety of subjects. He asks, "Read any new good books lately?"

Without pausing, Phil answers, "No. What's new and good to read? I've read many classics. I've studied some physics. I've read a lot of the philosophers. Most of the present day best seller list is dumbed down misinterpretations of eternal truths for the consumption of ingenues or jerk offs. Did you know that the best sellers of all time were written by Semites — the Bible, the Koran and the Torah? That's a good trivia question, 'What race of people has written more best sellers for a longer period than any other race?' The Semitic race is the answer. But the writings are about the poor Semites and their experiences. Not the grand stories of the Babylonians, Persians, Egyptians, Phoenicians and the like. And then there's the books by another Semite, Danielle Steel. She's the Jewess that is seventh on the all time best selling authors list. She writes for those desperate, horny housewives who get their labia minoras stuck with a lip grip on the special handicap door knobs. Occasionally they get caught by the suction of regu-

lar door knobs and have to wait till hubby gets home
to pry them loose. And then they blame poor hubby
for not performing enough to keep her off and away
from the lure of door knobs. Um. Danielle Steel. Isn't
a dildo sometimes called a 'steely dan'? So Steel Danielle is close. I wonder if she changed her name to at-
tract women perusing the book shelves? You know,
that subliminal stuff? She does provide those unique
under the toilet seat views I'm told. P.T Barnum had
it right with his, something like, you can't go broke
by underestimating public taste."

Gene pretended he was shocked. He said, "Gee,
I'm sorry I asked. I'm going to call you filthy Phil from
now on."

An amused Phil responds, "Sorry, Gene I just had
to gross you out. A little change of pace my boy."

Gene adds, "Actually, Danielle Steel is her real
name. And your Semitic best seller statement is pure-
ly a result of the Bible, Koran and Torah being translated into Latin and Greek. Then those translated
books were spread throughout the infrastructure of
the old sprawling Roman Empire. The decomposition
of Rome aided the spread of socialistic theocracies."

Phil answers, "That's an interesting take on Rome

and the spread of Semitic religions. Humans revert to their roots which are bound up in murky religions and fables pretty quickly when their secular governments fail. They can't stand to be alone in the dark. By the way, I'm writing another book."

An excited Gene asks, "What's its title? When did you start? What's it about? Why are you writing it?"

Phil is delighted to talk about his new project. He's happy with Gene's genuine interest. He answers, "Well to answer your last question first. I'm writing it because I know I can write better than I can read today. Whether I'm appreciated is another question. But I don't really care. I'm writing it for myself and I will be satisfied if that's the way it ends up. Of course I would be more happy if others enjoyed it also. We were talking about the best sellers list. This is my response to that wasteland. My book is a political fiction. It's about baby boomers getting together to overthrow the government. I haven't a title yet."

Gene asks in some amazement, "... 'baby boomers overthrowing the government?' Boy that's a mouthful. The last time I looked at my fellow boomers, the men looked and behaved like slugs. And the women boomers didn't want to make their husbands look bad by comparison so they became Mrs. Slug."

Phil fires back, "You have a point. But I have to write this book. I have to get my feelings off my chest and known to others. I can't stand the lies and or brainwashing on TV, radio and in print or on the internet. I have to respond. That's just the way I am."

Gene presses for the title, "And the title ... ?"

Phil with a stumped look says, "I have thought of a lot of possibilities. But so far none are right."

Gene answers, "Well, keep me posted. Can you give me an example of how and what you have written so far?"

Phil hesitates. He doesn't like to present something unless he's satisfied. And he's not sure his example will be in the final book. Anyway he says, "I'm not sure this piece will survive my final editing but here it is. First some context, I wanted my readers to be softened up to the idea of assassinating members of Congress and our leaders in the executive branch. Also, the tone I was going to use in delivering my message was to be palatable. You know, sugar coat a bitter pill. So that pointed to having our Congressional targets behave in such corrupt and barbaric ways so as to make the project of killing them not only acceptable but a duty and self defense. I don't want sympathy for someone I'm going to kill off. And to sugar coat the deadly deeds I was going to implant the whole thing in a dark farce, generating laughs while there's killing going on. Actually my biggest challenge was to portray members of Congress in a farce way. Farce is everyday and routine behavior for them. So I really had to go over the top to get my point across to the numbed electorate who were going to be my readers."

Gene nods his understanding and says, "Sounds like a good tactic. You should note that Sarah Palin is publishing her campaign memoirs. Your book won't get as many laughs as her's. Her life story is a natural farce. She won't know what you're talking about when you say farce either. She'll think that multiple effluvium. Please continue."

Phil continues in a story teller voice. He starts with a prologue, "As our farce opens, the players are on Air Force One. President Amos Yomama is increasingly drowsy after drinking a specially prepared drink from his Secretary of State Butch Bubba. Moments earlier he got word that Vice President Joe Bartender was found dead in Fort Marcy Park. That's the same park that Butch's husband, Clint Bubba's aid committed suicide also some years earlier. The Vice President's death was an apparent suicide. There were three shots to the head like Bubba's aid had. Also on the plane is Speaker Guida Facista-Cana. As per the Presidential Succession Act of 1947, Facista-Cana would become president if any thing happened to Yomama or the president pro teme of the Senate. Coincidentally the president pro teme of the Senate, ninety-two year old Senator Seth Buzzard was just rushed to the hospital in a coma. The causes of the collapse and coma were unknown. But coincidentally he was at a picnic with the Vice President at that same park when he swooned. He was not expected to regain consciousness. And if anything happened to Facista-Cana then Butch Bubba would become president. What was in that drink that Butch Bubba made for Yomama? Facista-Cana suspects something very bad and is visibly troubled by the sequence of improbable events happening when she's alone with Butch Bubba at 35,000 feet. Facista-Cana asks Butch,' What was in that drink?' Butch turns slowly. Her face looks like Linda Blair's in 'The Exorcist'. Her pants suit steams. Her vagina speaks, ' Now it's my turn'. Facista-Cana panics and reaches for a hidden gun and gut shoots Butch. The anti-Christ pops out of Butch's stomach and lands on the ground. It's the love child of the quarter-Jew Butch and a Cuban-Jew waiter. It was a quick affair. She met him in Miami while changing planes. Butch was even surprised at the fetus. She shows regret. She reaches out to the bearded child. But she then falls dead. The child scrambles to sanctuary in the toilet. He runs back out to get pen and paper for his best seller project. He slams the door shut. Facista-Cana slumps into a chair. She's exhausted. Suddenly, she hears what sounds like a zipper. Someone is walking towards her in mincing steps. It's Clint Bubba wearing a pilots cap. He has been on the plane all along and nobody knew. Bubba was wearing a fake blonde beard. He was the only pilot. The planes on automatic. His trousers are down around his ankles and they hobble his walk. He speaks,' Thanks for getting rid of the bitch. Will you make me vice president or will you do something else for me?' Facista-Cana is speechless. She gathers her wits and shoots Clint Bubba. He falls dead. She runs to check Yomama. She unbuttons his shirt and checks for a heart beat. He's dead. It must have been poison in the drink. She notices something very strange under his shirt. She gets her cell phone and calls her husband. Her husband picks up the phone. She speaks in a cool and business-like way, "Hi honey it's me. Is the market still open? Using the offshore accounts sell short a thousand S&P 500 futures contracts. Never mind. Put the order in now and then I'll tell you what happened." About thirty seconds pass. She speaks, "All done? That's great. Listen I haven't much time. I'm now president. Yeah, we got the empire back. Hail to the Senate and People of Rome. That's right, they're all dead. Would you believe that Yomama wears a genuine leopard skin outfit under his suit? Got to go. Call Goldman Fucks and tell them about the rumor of a coup. I'll give you two minutes and then I'll notify the events to the airport. Yeah, there going to have to talk me down. Cover the short before the close. I need a sandwich. Buy for now. What? Oh, yes. I'm going to tell 'em that Bubba and his wife did the killings and I was lucky to survive... "That's how far I have got. What do you think Gene?" asks a cautious Phil.

Gene stares at Phil for a very long moment. Then Gene asks in voice that has no emotion, "This is the message? Lookout they don't kill the messenger. I think it needs work. Pass the butter please."

Phil sheepishly offers, "I've another segment that softens peoples attitude towards racism. It will make them feel it's OK to be racist because you have to keep up with the competition. The segment demonstrates how the minorities are way ahead in practicing reverse racism and just straight racism. It depends on how stupid a person or how cowardly the person is that they are talking to. Do you want to hear it?

An impatient Gene hurriedly moves to another subject. "Maybe later Phil. You mentioned lawyers.

What about lawyers? I'm a lawyer. How about me? Try to keep it to an elevator trip length." said an intense Gene who obviously enjoys verbal sparing and conversations with purpose.

Phil jumps to the challenge. He's eager to reengage the conversation. He says, "Alright. Lawyers are the means of enforcement of all the many frivolous entitlements and presumptuous rights that have been extended to our democracy's citizens. The rights and entitlements have become more numerous than the barnacles on the bottom of 'Old Ironsides' and just like those barnacles they put a drag on the ship of states performance. But it's a full employment work project for lawyers. So they constantly dream up and lobby for more entitlements. Our Congress is infested with lawyers. The premise of the entitlements is that all are created equal. When in fact we are known by our differences. But there is no money in the truth. Lies are much more profitable albeit more expensive to sustain. How about this motto : ' Have laws will travel?'- like Richard Boone's ' Paladin ' TV series in the 1960s or 70s. I think the Federal Register is now 120,000 pages of fine printed rules and regulations. Lawyers are the only profession that get paid more for purposely delaying a resolution of a problem. Notice the twenty-five percent of our graduating class became lawyers. Half of them would successfully heist a hot stove while the other half would take notes on how it was done. Constructively, Americas legal paradigm is designed to delay justice. Which means that justice is denied. Which means that our legal system is effectively a restraint of trade. The laws arcane structure mandate delay, consequently the simplest case turns into an expensive billable affair which leads seamlessly to shake-down settlements. This low bar for succeeding as an attorney in general leads to more of the less bright and more larcenous lawyers prospering longer than anyone would possibly imagine. Where are the antitrust lawyers? They should refer to the Sherman Antitrust laws for the applicable provisions."

A smiling Gene talks as if he were speaking to a pupil that finally 'got it', "That was too long. But it was an acceptable exception to brevity because it was well said and almost entertaining in its message. But you want to get lawyers to police lawyers? Hello? Did you hear yourself?"

"Would you believe that I wanted to see if you're listening? We have to start somewhere. There's no honor among thieves. And this antitrust case could be hugely lucrative and would easily lead to a political career." answers a sly Phil.

"Do you think me larcenous or dumb?" asks Gene in a somewhat make or break their friendship way depending on the answer. Although in Gene's heart, he knows that Phil will continue to be his friend because Gene knows Phil will have a plausible explanation that will give Gene wiggle room to accept.

Phil becomes embarrassed and wants to continue Gene's friendship. But he's also honest and doesn't want to come off as either less of a friend or not honest when speaking. So he speaks honestly on how he feels. Let the chips fall where they may. Although he knows that Gene will understand and that there's really no chance in a breakdown in the long friendship. And Phil intends to give Gene and himself wiggle room to make sure there are no lingering resentments. Phil speaks in a slow deliberate cadence that is meant to be taken as the truth." Gene you are my friend. But your profession and my past profession are not noble endeavors. In my own case, trading stocks is selfish and depending on what I do with the profits I don't advance our species. In your case, lawyers are indeed compensated for delay. Now if you can make a compelling case why delay is good I'll buy lunch." Phil stared at Gene and Gene stared back. Both knew that both professions had its flaws. But their relationship was more important than ending a friendship over obvious moot points.

After a brief dramatic pause which maybe somewhat overly dramatic in its length, Gene spoke, "I have one question for you. If you ever get sued what will you do?

A suddenly relaxed Phil smiled broadly, perhaps too broadly, dropped his chin and rhetorically rolled over on his back with the response, "Touche. Why I'd call you, Gene, buddy boy."

Gene obviously pleased, took a sip of his drink and said with a magnanimous flair, "Thanks".

Phil wasn't through. With somewhat of a sneaky look on his face he said, "But now I have one question for you Gene. As you know some attorneys get one thousand dollars per hour win, lose or draw. That effectively makes access to justice limited to the rich. A nine millimeter bullet only costs ten cents. That makes a kind of justice both affordable and easily accessed. Do you think that in the not too distant future people might opt for the bullet in place of the lawyer? When they ask the question 'Who you gonna call when you want criminal busters?'"

Gene somewhat shocked and amused leaned back and said softly, "Touche. The score is tied."

Phil had a proud look and extended his left hand as per the fencing custom after a match. Fencers shake the un-gloved hands. He said, "Good bout."

Gene picked up the thread of the former main topic of health care. He said, "I have further information that you may not be aware of concerning health care cost drivers. My son-in-law is a practicing doctor. I've asked him about the role the threat of law suits or an actual law suit has in raising overall medical costs. He agrees with your observation. But according to him, an equal or even more of a factor in driving up medical care is the cost of complying with federal and state regulations. He says that for every one hour he spends caring for a patient, he or his staff spends another hour filling out forms for insurance companies, the feds and the state. That is very, very expensive. Please continue Phil."

And Phil did continue with an anxiety to move away from the solid point scored by Gene. But also he was relieved that a sticky situation was put away in a friendly way. Phil spoke, "You want succinct when people speak. Well to sum up our back and forth about health care reform and attorneys, I'll quote our second president John Adams. He put it best and briefly when he said, 'In my many years I have come to a conclusion that one useless man is called a disgrace, two are called a law firm and three or more are called a Congress'."

Gene smiled so as to deflect the knockout blow and said, "I know that quote. When did you hear it?"

Phil didn't dwell on the victory but responded, "Moving right along, minority issues didn't have to become a problem in this country. Our greedy white legal weenies and their license to steal inflamed and disturbed race relations unnecessarily by codifying personal taste. Race relations in its essence is about personal taste. And everyone knows or should know one should never argue or enforce taste. If people don't want to deal with other people that's their own business. The South had a problem with codifying tastes in some state and local laws. By statute they excluded blacks from certain places. Those laws should have been struck down. And they would have in time. But the Civil Rights activists, were not happy just to get those repressive laws off the books, they go on to make the same mistake that the South made by passing legislation that codified race relations. It took the form of quotas, affirmative action and it de facto removed a persons critical thinking and judg-ment as a reason for not hiring someone. That was pure mischief. But it was very lucrative purposeful, mischief for the attorneys. The nationwide black/

white race relations were better before Civil Rights legislation of the 60s. Desegregation would have happened eventually and in a non-violent way in time. Suppose the opposite were true? Suppose southerners in retaliation for the northern activists invasion came up to the Bay Area on buses and they brought along some willing black folks who didn't have a home in the South? Suppose the southerners and the black folks demanded that white neighborhoods set aside one house on each block for a black southern resident? How would that have effected the civil rights debate? Of course that eventually did happen with affirmative action, quotas and busing students. But it wasn't the southerners that did it. It was the mischievous attorneys and politicians again. They guaranteed themselves controversy with Civil Rights Acts. That meant a good income for years to come. How many blacks play dumb or are unnecessarily argumentative so they can game the system even more? They are the equivalent of our white weenie lawyers. Too many lawyers, too many people."

"Your point on lawyers is well taken. Even though you were unknowingly preaching to the choir." said a smooth Gene who felt somewhat in control of his friends ramblings. But he also notices Phil eager face and feels he's about to lose control of Phil and almost aborts his next question but asks it anyway,

"Don't you think the blacks needed a federal inter-
vention? Some of those laws breached or nudged up
against the Bill of Rights. Even if they were exploited
by greedy attorneys and politicians?"

Phil almost started before Gene finished his
question. It's like he rehearsed his answer. Gene was
correct in his apprehension. Phil sailed right into it.
"Question Gene. What cost is appropriate to fix a
problem? In other words is there a problem that re-
quires such a high price to fix that a particular solu-
tion must be abandon? The Civil War was related to
slavery and tangential economic and political issues.
Was the Civil War worth it? The Lincoln 1860 presidential victory and the republican control of Congress unnerved the South on slavery issues. Lincoln
and Congress talked about passing a law forbidding
slavery in newly added states. The South suspected it would be only a matter of time before Lincoln
would force abolition on current states. Which he
in fact did with the Emancipation Proclamation. At
that time slavery was legal. Lincoln and Congress'
threat of actions would violate states rights. Concur-
rently there was a worldwide movement for abolition
that was both non-violent and successful. But Lincoln and Congress didn't want to wait for a non violent revolution. Jefferson Davis and his Confederacy
were unnerved by the prospect of an arbitrary end

to slavery which would have plunged the South into an economic depression. Confederate troops fired on Union forces at Fort Sumter in South Carolina. Lincoln responded in kind and the rest is history. Lincoln and the Union forces prevailed. The war and scorched earth policy on the South was hailed as a great moral victory. That is in spite of the facts that the total deaths approximate 700,000. That's more deaths than the totals of the Revolutionary War, Spanish-American, two World Wars, Viet Nam and the present Iraq and Afghanistan mistakes. Lincoln and Davis easily did more damage than any foreign foes to America's best men and women. And in spite of those gruesome facts the perception lingers and has grown that Lincoln was a great president and Davis was a great patriot by their respective partisans. Who was morally right? The South had the current law on its side. Lincoln and the republicans had the moral high ground. But the cost of 700,000 made both their positions unworthy to rack up such carnage. Amazingly to this day nobody mentions the 700K number. I guess they're OK with the number as long as its not their life. Public judgment and values sometimes are a cesspool. And many still think that variations on that kind of disastrous economic and social affirmative action should be extended to minority groups including illegals no matter what it does to the social fabric or the economy of the coun-

try. To answer your question, the blacks had grievances pre-Civil War. But they were not worth 700,000
dead. The Civil War was a war of choice. No choosers
of war should win lest it become a bad habit. Time
would have cured and normalized the differences
without such tremendous violence. Legal slavery was
on its way out for two reasons. Technology was just
around the corner in the picking of cotton and the
non violent abolition of slavery was gaining momentum. And finally to answer your question, Professor
Ray, so too was the Civil Rights Act too costly a piece
of legislation to all of America to this day. The Souths
problem was local and should have been worked out
locally. It didn't need a national fix."

Gene spoke, "Phil you mentioned earlier that you
had written a piece on making racism more acceptable. It was from your farce. I need some laughs. Fire
away."

A eager Phil said, "Sure Gene. It's based on the
fact that Yomama moved his mother-in-law into the
White House. Her name is Ruby Begonia. She runs
into Yomama's Chief of Staff, Israel (Izzy) Loverat who
is a Zionist Jew. The story opens with both of them
outside the Oval Office.

Ruby speaks with an air of authority, 'Hey boy,

where's my son-in-law?'

Izzy immediately resents the tone of voice and doubles her insult, 'Shouldn't you be in uniform? There's someone at the door.'

Ruby catches on real fast. She says with relish, 'It's Jeremiah Wright coming to call, Jew boy. And you know what he thinks of your kind. I dated Jerry for awhile. He got his opinions of heebs like you from me.'

The gloves are off. Izzy fires, 'Listen you tub of shit, don't pull rank on me. My slave credentials are longer than yours.'

Ruby responds quickly, 'And rightly so. You should be segregated and enslaved. We Africans were minding our own business in our own country. Hear that asshole? We had a country when we were forced onto slave ships. What's on your head ass wipe?

Izzy is steaming. He blurts out, 'It's a yarmulke. You ignorant cow. It's a head covering of distinction.

A coy Ruby says, 'Why don't you cheap Jews pay a little more and get a real hat like the fedora "King-fish" wore in "Amos 'n Andy"? That yami is just the remnants of a bigger hat. That's the stuff they threw away when they made a fedora.'

Izzy offers a truce with a conciliatory voice. He says 'I haven't got time to bicker. We both know why we're here. It's to get whitey. So can we work together?'

Ruby answers, 'I'll think on it'.

Gene laughs. He says, "That's good. I liked that. It's truthful therefore it meets the first requirement of a funny story."

A happy Phil says, "Thanks Gene."

Gene asks, "I wonder where people like Rut Lintball would stand on the Civil War? Where would Clint Bubba and his cunt wife stand? What would Yomama think about the costs and the rewards of the Civil War? That would be a hell of a question for presidential or congressional candidates."

Phil thought a moment and said, "That would be the litmus test. If any candidate answered that the Civil War was justified that should be enough to disqualify him or her for office. Because it just would be a matter of time before the caricature effect that happens with everything would produce another civil war. And such a government would continue our national policy of preemptive war. I think there is a connection between the Civil War and our present preemptive war policy. If the North would have lost or not chosen to fight the South, things might have been a lot different. Winning a war almost guarantees seeking other wars of choice which surely leads to inevitably losing a big war eventually."

A somewhat confused Gene wants a confirmation of what Phil said, "So you believe that losing a war is better than winning one?"

An eager Phil says, "Yes. Winning wars of aggression only guarantee more arrogance and more wars of aggression. In the end one country can't fight the whole world. Particularly now, with the proliferation of lethal weapons that only need one person to operate. So in the end the aggressor nation is crushed from all sides. The only way to win is to win the peace. Either by avoiding war or by killing the occupiers once they move in. Just look at Iraq. We won the invasion but lost everything else and it's still not over."

Gene looked satisfied with Phil's reasoning. But he wasn't too sure he agreed with Phil's conclusion. But Gene moved on, "You mentioned too many people. Maybe you need another Negroni first? Waiter. Two more drinks please." Gene questions Phil as if he were cross examining someone at a trial. "Aren't you really a misanthrope?"

Phil answers in a matter of fact manner, "No. But I am being swayed somewhat. These traffic jams and increasingly more jams are living reminders and it will get worse. Haven't you become progressively somewhat more misanthropic? There's a time for everything. That's the way of things. At almost 7 billion, where's your red line? We are looking up the rear end of bugs and recently discovered mammals because we just clear cut their habitat and discovered them clinging to life. The bugs and animals might ask 'What the fuck are you doing? And where did you come from? Please leave us alone.' It seems I'm running into more and more people who agree with my evaluations. We are all talking about it now. But what's next when the time for talk is over?"

Gene asks in a challenging way, "Alright I'll bite. How many people should be on the planet?"

Phil answers with the demeanor and voice pace of a professor who is outlining the upcoming course to the newly enrolled students, "The optimum human global population should be approximately

250,000,000. That was the population between 500 B.C. And 500 A.D. Which coincided with the high classical periods for Eastern and Western cultures. The pre-Socratics and Eastern philosophers intuitively described the workings of the cosmos. Pretty much what followed was taking those observations of physical principles and constructing machines and software that effectively mimic those phenomena. Consequently our sophisticated tools have made many, many of us redundant as producers of work. Consequently, approximately 70% of us are only valuable as consumers. Munch, munch, munch. Many have defaulted into choosing Type 2 diabetes as a lifestyle. The government supports that lifestyle. That's pathetic and constructively evil. I plead guilty to the under worked category in these later years. But I'm not smug about it. I guess I need some really compelling challenge to get me humming again and sweating again. Fencing fulfills some of that need and outlet but it's still not life or death. There's nothing like a life or death struggle to focus the mind and to get creative."

Gene agreed, "Yes Phil, we are largely munchers. I wonder if Homer's Lotus Eaters in the Odyssey was about our type? Anyway, you may or may not know it. But that same approximate figure of 250,000,000 was arrived at by calculating our species needs versus what the planet naturally and easily produces. It was a study on our balance in nature requirements. The study was presented to the Royal Society in London or some venue like that about 7-8 years ago. I forget who the scientist was but according to his figures the human could sustain itself indefinitely at that static number."

A surprised and pleased Phil said, "I didn't know about that study. So culturally and logistically there is a nexus at 250. Funny how if it works at one level it probably works at another."

"But there's not much you can do about planning for that nexus at this lunch." Gene cracks.

Phil answers with a prediction and obligation, "That's true. But since we are aware that there should be an approximate finite or optimum population number, then it filters out many unsustainable growth schemes. I'm not alone. The environmental movement at its roots is a culling of the human to a more balanced number. For now it's humane. But at some point in its evolution it will become a caricature and turn aggressively active. That will be interesting to see how that develops. What form and what kind of leader and what kind of methods will come forward? Or will disease take everything out of our

hands? AIDS looks like a comer. Genocidal wars?
They've never stopped. An extra terrestrial event?
Double zero does come up on the roulette wheel. My
hunch is that catastrophic change will come in the
form of someone who will be charming. The person
doesn't need looks but they would help. The charmer's biggest asset will be straight talk. He/she won't
lie. Truth will be the gold standard in today's 'pal-
ace of lies' to quote the devil in the dream sequence
from Shaw's 'Man and Superman'. The charmer will
only need events as a backdrop to his truthful words,
so as to back light the words. But the failure of all
charmers in the past is not knowing when to stop.
Most ideas have some merit. But all ideas become
a disaster when administered in too great a portion
and in a sloppy way."

A visibly impressed Gene agrees and adds "The
future points to great political storms. The affairs of
man are like 'a sea that always rages'. It's written
somewhere. Politics has gotten very mean. Nobody
smiles, nobody is cordial and politicians think if they
only got their way it would be better. Compromise
isn't necessary because both parties are paid too
much for endless argument. But nothing lasts forev-
er. Even raging seas expend their energy and seek re-
pose. If one looks at chaos as the end of one regimen
and the beginning of another then this could be a fun

time in shaping what is to follow. But change is going to have to come from outside the system. I'm tired of voting for change and getting more of the same but only more costly and more intrusive. An economic collapse will finally enforce a priority in spending by our government. And with that collapse a complete dissolution of of our type of government would be possible and most welcome by many. A lot of those wasteful and counterproductive policies will have to be abandoned. But then trade wars or hot wars become increasingly likely to bolster the economy."

Phil jumps in, "Just think, Congress will finally have to spend less. Probably the main reason why people go into politics is to privately get paid and benefit from allocating public government funds to special interests. It's consenting adults carving up tax payers. Campaign reform? Earmarks reform? Not ever. Special interests pay pennies for mega dollar contracts or to change laws that change the financial or regulatory landscape so to make stealing legal and with the governments blessing. How much money is kicked back secretly to members of Congress through sweet heart business deals that are never discovered? And if things get slow congress supports a hot war to kick over an anemic economy. If someone had a gun pointed at you while they were stealing your wallet, you could kill 'em in self defense. What's the difference when Congress steals a lot more than pocket money and then sends you and your neighbor and your children into a war zone just so they can get reelected?" Says an agitated Phil.

Phil follows up on his congressional and politicians tirade, "How about those union thugs at SEIU? They remind me of Hitler's Brown Shirts but without the breeding. I'll bet half of them have criminal records in Mexico. The democrats bus them around to threaten folks at town hall meetings and political rallies. Note the 'I' in the SEIU? It stands for 'international'. That's a garbage can full of attitude for a group that mostly sweeps floors. They resemble the seeds of a worldwide communist workers party."

Gene turns to metaphor, "Yomama is our first minority president. He's a cartoon of the children that were quasi-fathered by the artificial insemination of the Great Society. The next president will be more of a caricature. It's like an arms race. All life forms move towards caricature including the life form of democracy and its political template. First the democrats elect caricature. Then the energized base of the republicans elect a cartoon. Morons with banners shouting and shoving with no one thinking or listening."

"'Quasi-artificial insemination of the Great Society'", Phil turns the phrase slowly over, "That conjures up an image. I like that characterization. That's poetic. All those programs certainly boosted child births. And those children were raised with a philosophy of deserved entitlement. It's kind of like a kings divine right only this right is for the bottom of society. It's very expensive and subject to much abuse. I don't believe in hereditary monarchies and I certainly don't believe in hereditary slave affirmative action. Any of the West African slaves that were sold into slavery by their tribesmen in the 17th century and ended up in the U.S. should call themselves lucky. What opportunity were the slaves torn from in Africa? I heard Yomama's wife speak the other day. Boy does she fall from his skills at speaking. She reminds me of the 18th century philosopher David Hume's comments on the so-called sophistication of the black Jamaicans. It happened that a traveling friend of Hume wrote a letter about the Jamaicans to him. Some years later Hume visited Jamaica to see for himself. He wrote his friend back and in a nutshell said he saw no difference between a well trained parrot and a native Jamaican. Both spoke perfect English but neither knew what they were talking about. Et tu Yomamas? That Scotsman Hume was great. Do you think we will get a trade war?"

Gene asks with some shock, "Didn't she go to Harvard? God, what's next?"

Phil answers with more than some sarcasm but made passable with much levity, "She sure did. What's next? I'll tell you. I understand that a Jewish advocacy group is going to apply a parrot to be Dean of Black Studies at Harvard next year. They reason that since neither the prospective dean or the students know what they're talking about it will be OK. They already have an extensive legal team assembled to claim discrimination if the parrot is not accepted. It's all a straw man or straw bird legal ploy to tap into a new theater of controversy between Gentile and Semitic relations. It's the old one-two tactic used by the minorities. Send a black through an obstacle and see if he comes back bloody. If so then adjust your tactic. Wait until the blacks are safely brought through the ordeal then it's safe to send a Jew. No matter what happens the culture will be trashed again and the odd balls will feel more comfortable."

Gene hooting with laughter says, "Say what?" Warrior Yomama patronizes the military-industrial-complex. In return the lobbyists throw billions of recycled federal contract money into Yomama's re-election/slush fund account. Yomama responds by sending children from other families to Afghanistan.

The troops are well meaning but I fear they are naive. They think they can win a fight for another's meager home. But they don't realize that meager home is all the Afghan has. Yomam's difference with the republicans on war making is only a matter of degree. His is more bite sized. The republicans gorge. They both favor weapons used by bullies and cowards like drone aircraft and laser-guided bombs that also kill many innocents. All those innocents that are killed leave behind grieving families. They in turn join the resistance against us and NATO. Our way of war is a breeder reactor for more, never ending war. If an Afghan threw his shoe at this Yomama that contained an I.E.D., would it be murder or would he be acting in self-defense by saving many Afghan lives?" Gene answered his own question, "Natural law would say self defense. Probably strict interpretation of Afghan law would condone the act also. But the U.S. law would allow killing the thrower on the spot. Not because it's moral but because it could be done and done easily. No matter what scenario, somebody would follow Yomama who would continue the war. America thrives on war. The Iraqi that threw his shoe at President Shrub got sentenced to 5 years in prison. But he was just released by popular demand. Of all the crimes Shrub and his Veep Chainsaw committed there was only one guy who was brave enough to physically assault one of them in person. How fuckin' sad is that?

Boy, by implication that makes many people not only redundant but also shows them to be cowardly and easily made to be slaves."

Phil adds in haste, "The fuckin' Shrub was an affirmative action, moron, white boy at Yale. I think Yomama's wife can even speak better than the Shrub. The guy should be tried for war crimes. Somebody should handle his case the way they handled Lincoln's case. That would be a powerful message."

Gene looks at Phil and asks in a serious tone, "Do you believe in assassinations?"

Phil looks at Gene in an equally serious way and answers, "Of course I believe in assassinations. Look how many lives would have been saved over the years if certain certifiable bad guys were terminated. And if war wasn't averted, at least it would have been delayed somewhat and the circumstances might have changed over time enough to avert a war. If we think that war crime trials are appropriate after a war. Why then wouldn't killing war mongers before a war be a more noble endeavor?"

"You have a point." answers Gene. He can't believe that his charming friend has just made a cogent argument for assassination that he could support and maybe even commit. But is it his friend or is it the times that make assassinations seem attractive. It's probably the times. His friend could be the charmer who speaks the truth that they spoke of earlier. Will Phil act. And if he acts will he know when to stop?

Phil asks, "Is Yomama a minority president or majority president? Minority in race yes, but he got a majority of the votes. There are still many people who think Washington has the answers despite year-ly evidence to the contrary. By the way, technically the first minority president was Clint Bubba a.k.a. Ozark Caligula. He won with only 43% of the vote. That was compliments of Red Parrot. Parrot split the majority. I had an elevator ride with Bubba once. It was in Washington at the Mayflower Hotel. He gets in with his Secret Service body guards. He bellows out, 'Good Morning. How are you today?' He comes on like it was my lucky day and that I would cherish and pass on the experience to friends and family for years to come. Well I deflated him. I said, 'Can't you ever be quiet?' He looked at me like a scolded hound. He folded his hands and looked down at the floor. I thought later I should have told him his fly was down and there were drip marks on his size 13 shoes. I can't stand that phony fucker. He reminds me of the Andy Griffith character, 'Lonesome Rhodes' in 'A Face In The Crowd'. Both are egotistical frauds."

"Will we have a trade war you asked?" Gene remembers Phil asked earlier. "That would complete
the full circle repetition of the Great Depression experience. We seemed to have chosen to repeat all
the other mistakes that lead up to the Great Depression already. We repealed Glass-Steagall and
let the banks back into the securities and insurance
business. That was mostly to blame for our recent
financial meltdown. And now we have some healthy
banks take over weak and toxic investment bankers
to make the next bubble burst worse than this past
one. Why not a trade war? That's were SEIU comes in
and the recently refortified auto worker unions. FDR
made the same kind of mistakes with protectionism
for the industrial base and propping up unions at
the start of the down turn in 1929. It only exacer-
bated the problem into a full blown depression. And
Yomama with help from Congress is doing the same
thing. There shouldn't be a Big Three American auto
industry because it can't be sustained. There probably should be only a big one. Subsidizing the industry for the sake of the workers is illogical. It only
makes the recovery of three more difficult. But this
is the way of politicians. Policies don't have to be ef-
fective but only appear to be. Heaven forbid that you
tell the voters the truth. Let the stupid voters find out
on their own. Meanwhile the reps in Congress will
continue to draw salaries above and below the table

despite poor performance." says a jaded Gene.

Phil adds, "You're right on. It's the damn NAZI and Fascist playbook all over again. Our government together with the unions and the industrialists running everything. Healthcare, schools and what's left of the culture through ministries of the personal taste police." says Phil coldly. He continues in a stream of consciousness, "If Yomama gets part of his transition done and then is kicked out by the voters, the republicans will take over with the promise to dismantle it but instead will build out and use the Fascist/NAZI political infrastructure for their own brand of mischief. The trade war imbalances almost will certainly cause another war because it will deepen the recession into a depression. *Deja vu* the 1930's. But this time the war weapons may well bring a finality to us—the frivolous primate. It's like the metaphysics of repeating history will be followed no matter what party is in control. Mulholland, the engineer who piped water in from the Owens Valley to bring life to the dry Los Angeles area said prophetically, 'We are doomed by our success'. He knew the draining of the Owens Valley in favor of a sprawling LA was not an improvement on the original landscape. Our technology enables us to do a great many things, almost magical things. But technology does not provide the wisdom as to whether it should be done."

"We are still stuck with the same outcomes because we never changed from that vengeful and greedy beast that we started out as. 'Forbidden Planet', the 1950s classic sci-fi movie, was a masterpiece on this subject. Have you seen that film?" Gene asked and recommended with his tone of voice.

"I haven't. I'll check out on Netflix. Oh look who just came in. It's a Zionist Senator," said a distracted Phil.

Gene replies in a cautionary way but it was too late, "I think she heard you. She's coming over."

Senator Silver speaks, "You guys should keep your voices down and show some respect. I may go to management."

Phil slams back, "Aren't you a Zionist? It's not like I called you a cunt? What's your problem?"

"My name is Senator Judith Silver asshole. Never mind if I'm a Zionist. I know that is an anti-Semitic slur. What's your name? Are you an Italian anarchist? You look like a grease ball. Contempt of Congress is a criminal offense that you can go to jail for or be fined. "The senator replies leaning into Phils face. She's hoping to scare Phil with a bluff. Saliva wells up in the corners of her mouth.

"Get out of my face. My name is legion for I am many and yes I am Italian. We Romans knew how to handle you troublemakers. For the record, I don't have contempt for Congress. I just have contempt for the criminals that run Congress. I know it's not entirely your fault that you are a Zionist. The blame is rightfully your mothers. Zionist mothers lie a lot. And don't give me that anti-Semitic crap either. There are Semites that I do support. In particular, I support the Palestinians. But I don't support Zionists. They are the black sheep of the Semitic race. Their basic problem is that they never really had a country of any consequence to begin with. They mostly roamed when they weren't being rounded up and enslaved. Consequently they never had a worthwhile culture and so they don't know how to behave in civilized societies. You people came and then locks went on doors and the airways filled up with lies." Phil mocks with high affectation determined to infuriate the senator. He also is aggressively studying the senators face with the intent of possibly insulting physical design flaws. This was next if she doesn't get out of his face.

Silver goes ballistic. All of a sudden she is struck with the memories of how the Jews were rounded up in the past. Thoughts of the Holocaust, Himmler and

Goebbels flooded into her mind. Was this the start of that cycle all over again? So far America was the only country that hadn't rounded up the Jews. Was that about to change?" She almost screeches in a whisper, "How dare you?"

Phil barely pauses and continues with a new level of intensity. It's as if Phil taps into his Roman roots, "When you can get past acting like a Zionist zealot and an Israeli operative then maybe I will stop speaking spontaneously and honestly about what I see. Aren't you a bag lady for Israel? Don't you sprinkle back small percents of the U.S. foreign aid cash that goes to that illegitimate country each year to some members of Congress? You know the ones. The ones who voted for the Israeli foreign aid in the first place. Shame on you and shame on Congress. Incidentally you shouldn't showcase your hairy arms. And that cheap dress, get it through the mail?"

Silver is red in the face. She wants to slap him. She thinks again and purposely tips Phil's water glass. It partially sprays both men. "Fuck you, you bigot. Israel is a glorious country given to the Israelites by God. The Wailing Wall is proof of our countries historical existence. Its history dates back thousands of years ago. I'm going to talk to the management if you don't leave this instant."

"Fuck me? Fuck you. Go ahead, talk to Darius. He's an Iranian. Another race you are insulting. By the way your mother lied. Israel was created in 1947 with a rigged/bribed United Nations vote that partitioned Palestine. That doesn't sound like god's work to me. It was the collaborative work of a hat salesman who became president, Harry Truman and his super Zionist buddy, Bernard Baruch. It's all in 'O' Jerusalem' by Collins and Lapierre. I advise reading it. Stop spreading lies about your history. Israel should be a theme park. But not in the Mideast. Not here either. How about a virtual Israel on the web? Oh yeah, before I forget, tell your mother that the guy at the restaurant thinks that the Wailing Wall was only a abandoned Babylonian warehouse. The Israelites occupied the derelict building in a sit-in. You remember, like some of the anarchist Jews did at U.C. Berkeley in those admin buildings in the 1960s. Hey, before you rush away and wipe your mouth, ask another Zionist senator if she remembers Gary, Larry and Gordon and the many other hounds at ABC News, KGO and KSFO at the Domino Club bar in the 70s? Why did she never have a ride home? Take a hike. And take this with you. Before their were Nazis there were only Germans. Likewise before there were Zionists there were only Jews. But before there were Nazis there were Zionists. The Greeks had a word that was the best advice to you people, 'moderation'.

Take the advice and avoid another Holocaust."

The Senator gives them the finger and walks away in a huff.

A visibly nervous Gene whispers, "Phil, calm down. Waiter, can you sop this water up please."

Phil answers, "Fuck her. She and her husband own two homes locally and other properties far and wide. They have an estimated net worth of $50,000,000. Her senators salary can only cover the property tax on one of her showplace homes. How do they do it? She has been in politics her whole life and he kind of pimps her or she uses him as a business agent. Whatever. Oh yeah, I almost forgot. Have you noticed the little cultural/religious war in our neighborhood?"

"What do you mean?", asks Gene in a calmer voice. He hopes that Phil will become calmer also.

"Well, Temple Emmanuel has added a 24/7 armed guard and a metal detector. Across the street at Arguello at Lake Street is St. John's, a Protestant church. It has a large banner proclaiming that this is St. John's Presbyterian Church. The banner also proudly includes that the church is, 'OPEN-SAFE-

REAL.' Isn't that a kick? The Presbyterians are leading the worldwide Israel divestiture movement."

Gene reports, "It looks like Darius is not going to
throw us out, despite Silver's red face, gestures and
elevated voice. They are not impressing him. Those
old Jew broads are like Pit bulls. She reminds me
of a joke Milton Berle told many years ago. For me
Berle was the best joke teller. Bare with me, trying
to do a Berle joke is very presumptuous. Anyway the
setting is in the Catskills They call that the Jewish
Alps. Jews from Manhattan travel there for summer
vacation. Entertainers follow and do the Borsht Belt
Circuit as they call it. So the story goes, a middle
age guy is laying by the pool. He's pale with no tan.
A older Jewish lady comes from the hotel lobby and
inspects to see if there are any prospects for love interest. Her husband died some years ago. She walks
slowly and observes all carefully. Not unlike she's
picking fruit or vegetables from a bin. She arrives at
the pale newcomers chaise lounge. She speaks with
more than a hint of a measuring, inquiring yet demanding Yiddish accent, ' Hi. Did you just arrive?'
The man somewhat startled from his peaceful state
says, 'Yeah.' Well the 'Yeah' was enough for her. Add
in that he was breathing normally and somewhat attractive. So she is now his fast friend. 'Where did you
come from? My name is Marcy'." He doesn't immedi-

ately respond in the hope that she will move along. He decided to pass on her after a quick glance at the lady. She continues, 'Would you like to have lunch with me?' He doesn't answer. ' Gee you are so pale'. He answers, 'No lunch.' in such a way so to try to give her the message that he has no interest in her, lunch or her opinions. She stays put. She won't go away. She just stares longingly. 'Where do you come from. Do you want to have dinner with me tonight?' Well that did it. The man opens his eyes props himself on his elbows and says, 'I've been in jail for the past twenty years for murdering my wife. I used an ax. I was doing 50 to life at Sing Sing but I was released early because I'm dying from pancreatic cancer." She answers immediately and undaunted, ' So you're single?'

Phil laughs loudly. Then he almost screams, "Let's Kill Members of Congress." He catches himself screaming and becomes self conscious and embarrassed. In a calmer and lower voice he asks Gene, "How about that title for my new book? What do you think Gene? It just came out of me. I had to say it. Wouldn't it be a real pleasure to unleash those long suffocated feelings I have through raw prose in my book? Just write a novella about killing the whole fuckin' bunch of them. But who will do it? How will it be done? Should I start it? Would it be worth it?" Phil speaks as if he's been transformed. Not raving, not drunk but like someone who has found his voice. It's like Phil experienced an epiphany. He found his voice and is at peace. It's all clear now. He's become whole. But is it an author musing about a plot or is it a revolutionary Phil in real time with a real dark plan? Phil probably doesn't know either which is more applicable.

A shocked, embarrassed, somewhat amused and confused Gene immediately tries damage control on his seemingly out of control friend, "Are you fuckin ' nuts? Phil, pipe down. You sound like the Howard Beale character in 'Network' when he gets up from his chair in the broadcast booth and proclaims to his audience, 'I want you all to get up and go to the window and say, I'm mad as hell and not going to take it any more '. You can think it but you can't shout it in a public place. The people think you're serious. They don't know it's a book title. Hell you sound serious. It sounded like a call to arms."

Phil's voice was loud enough to turn heads in his direction. An instant poll of the faces showed all were entertained or intrigued by the novel question. None of the faces reflected revulsion or dismissal out of hand. Some actually looked like they had some contributing ideas on how and why it should be done.

Some almost instinctively got up from their chairs to join the men at their table. Certainly all wanted to hear more. Phil moderated his voice. He and Gene chuckled while waving acknowledgment to the on-lookers.

"Why can rappers advocate homicide and rape? Why can Congress organize preemptive war? Why do white men get blamed for putting criminal, black morons in jail? Why can't I say 'Let's Kill Members of Congress' in public." Phil answers with the voice of a child asking his parents to explain a decision. But with an unmistakable undercurrent of an adult challenge to his friend who sounds like a child parroting instructions from an adult. Phil is asking his friend to grow up.

Gene rushes to answer, "Remember you're a white male who has to endure some emasculation for the sake of the greater multi-cultural society. Phil you are in a highly civilized country and you can't say things like let's kill members of congress in public. Writing a book is a different venue and context. But show restraint in public". Gene thought how awkward I sound. He asked himself if he really believed what he was preaching to Phil. Or was he so brainwashed that his response was involuntary?

Phil gets a hold of himself. "Don't give me that multicultural stuff. I'm a minority, remember, but the press and Congress treats me like a plantation owner. But I'll soften the title. How about, 'Who Is Killing Members Of Congress?' What do you think now? This is about a book I'm writing. It's a political fiction. Granted it's not a love story but it's only a book. Although it sounds like you nurture some dark revolutionary thoughts along those lines by the way you responded."

A more relaxed Gene responds, "That's much more acceptable. I would buy that title. It's more like the Socratic method of discovery. Ask questions before you believe what people say."

Darius, the owner of Sam's, walks to the table. He speaks in his usual tone. He's seems to be unaffected by Senator Silver's melt down. "Hi guys. How's lunch? Can I get anything for you?"

"No, Darius. Everything is great as per usual. I hope we didn't lose you a customer?" said a solicitous Gene.

"Not at all. It's a free country. But I did promise the senator that I would visit your table and warn you about further unpleasantness. Consider this a good will visit and nothing more." said a very sincere Darius.

"Thank you Darius. Does she come in often?" Asked Phil.

"Yeah. When Congress is not in session, she comes in everyday. You could set your watch within 3-5 minutes when she will come through the doors. Her office is down the block. She walks here." Darius responded while keeping an eye on the door where two people just walked in. "I got to hop boys. Enjoy the lunch." He walked away briskly.

Phil and Gene look at each other and were both pleased that Darius was OK and that they were still OK with Darius.

Gene asks Phil, "Where were we?" Pretending that he didn't remember. Then he says, "Where's the setting for your book? Who's involved? Do you have accomplices?"

An unaffected Phil picks up right were he left off. He's picked up some encouragement from his normally dispassionate and brilliant friend by the interest that Gene is displaying. And Phil is encouraged by what his friend didn't say. He didn't say it was wrong to write about killing members of Congress. Phil speaks, "The setting is going to be right here. It will be me and someone else having a freewheeling conversation about our beliefs and fears. No PC. Just the truth. It will be like our conversations. In fact I'm going to model my companion on you. I won't use your name or give away your identity. But I need some foil to bring out interesting talk. Conversations are always interesting to people who buy books or go to the movies. Ever ride a bus and listen to two people talking? Of course you could move or think about something else but you probably stayed put and got some free entertainment. What makes it entertaining and interesting is its truth. Never mind their opinions are ones that you don't support. The talk is real and consequently it's interesting. So a conversation with me and maybe some one like you about topical subjects told in an interesting and honest way should sell some books. At least I'll feel better for the exercise." Phil laid out his outline.

Gene listened intently and spoke, "Do you think a civilized group of boomers would be interested in revolution or talk about uncivilized acts?"

Phil answered with conviction, "No, no Gene this is not a civilized country any more. I think the Civil War precluded a civilized description of America. But

actually the U.S. definitely became uncivilized country when Clint Bubba attacked Serbia in the 1990's.
Serbia did nothing to America. Many people in power
noticed that the American public didn't object to that
murderous act. And so the modern age of American
imperialism and aggression was born. Remember the
Project For The New American Century? That's what
that organism from hell was all about. The Shrub /
Chainsaw administration tore up peace treaties with
Russia before 9/11. But when 9/11 happened, that
was the excuse to make preemptive war our national
policy. And the first target was the hapless Iraqi people. As far as I'm concerned it's every man for himself
as long as there is a preemptive war policy in the
U.S. I personally feel it's my duty to stop Congress
and the executive from aggressive war making on
my behalf. If someone killed Hitler early on it would
have been called murder by most. But after he did
his deeds, people were waiting in line to righteously
kill Adolf and get a medal for it. I'll make it simple for
you Gene. As long as there is a preemptive war policy in American I feel compelled to stop all that support that policy. Keeping silent or passive is not an
option. Because then I'm complicit." He spoke with
much conviction. "What do you think Gene? Are you
OK with preemptive war in your name?" Phil stares
at Gene and waits for an answer.

"I don't like it. Murdering reps in Congress and people in the executive branch is a whole lot to swallow after this lunch. Wait a minute, is this for real or is this a book rehearsal question?" demands Gene.

Phil answers with a challenge in his voice, "It's about my book. But does it matter? Just give me your honest answer. I thought you did that all the time? This is not a screen test reading. Can't we talk about any subjects academically? Relax and forget about my book. That's my burden. Think of your answers as method acting if that helps. But method acting draws on real life emotions and experiences. So in short, just give me honest answers even if they ask you to speculate on crimes that you would not personally commit or would condone. OK? Get in the spirit of it so I can get material."

Gene answers with a more relaxed voice, "OK. I get it now. Just conversation and as usual no editing. It's about getting material for the book."

Phil picks it back up, "How would people behave to a rash of dead, missing or scandal ridden members of Congress? How about we start a real time democratic election and/or de-election government? Don't be satisfied with waiting to see the results of a vote tally? Make sure your vote is counted. Forget rigged votes. Forget Diebold voting machines problems. Let your congressman hear from you! Political disposals are not murder. When done with the best intentions of the voter it is just a political statement. They are much like the war votes on launching preemptive wars. These wars were not described as brutal aggression or mass murder. The preemptive war was sold as life-saving legislation. The votes were done according to a political process that is backed up by long recorded beautiful prose that has become de facto mumbo jumbo. Ergo if our leaders can legally commit mass murder in our name aren't we the voters entitled to some maintenance disposals of our own to mitigate what's been done and to prevent another preemptive war and criminal mass murder? After all they made us all accomplices in their mass murder of many innocent Iraqis. Are you OK with murder as long as Congress does it following parliamentary procedure? But you deny yourself the duty of killing members of Congress because you don't have the moral authority even when it's in self defense and to stop further preemptive war?"

Gene thought to himself. Phil has made some accurate points. Blood lust in all humans lives very close to the surface. After all we are the main predator on the planet. Not only have we killed entire species but we continually drive all other kinds of flora and fauna to the brink of extinction. And we kill in so many ways. It could be active killing with technology or passive poisoning with our emissions. One example are the massive dams on mighty rivers so we can turn on television but then mute most of the junk. Meanwhile millions of fish die or suffer so we can use a mute button. We cannot afford dead end technology. But what keeps us all going strong is that some presumptuous fool said we were created in the image of god. That's some kind of evil god who creates one species to piss on the rest of creation. One thing about the word 'god' that is for sure. Spelled backwards it becomes 'dog'. And that's giving the dog the worst of the comparison."

Gene responded in an affected ceremonial fashion, "Let me mark the event. Di Caesari crosses his own kind of Rubicon today at this hour and at Sam's. Phil had lunch... Then he went forth... Then he saw... Then he conquered. I'd better get you to sign the menu and other ephemera for an Antiques Roadshow down the road. On second thought maybe not. It could turn out to be used as Peoples Evidence against the accused Philip Di Caesari. But to answer your question, if I'm OK with murdering members of Congress, I'm not OK with it. I see your points. But right now we live in paradigm of law and procedures. Julius Caesar crossed the actual river Rubicon about 50 B.C.. Roman law prohibited a general from leading his legions to the environs of Rome. His breach set him up as an Imperial ruler and the Roman Empire followed. He broke Roman law and it's never been the same nor has it been any different since that time. Will you make the same mistakes as the people you are trying to remove from office did? Or will you have the self discipline to avoid that error? Caesar became a mass murderer in the name of The Senate and People of Rome. Remember those initials — SPQR? Will you really dismantle Washington and central government. Power corrupts. Will you be the exception?"

Phil answered with confidence, "As an author and as me, I will not make those errors."

Gene looked about and said, "It looks like an idea who's time has come if these folks around us are to be believed. Book or no book! An outbreak of dead or missing Congressional members might be welcome by something approaching a super majority. Nobody really likes politicians. People prefer a blood sport with politicians. What's to like? They are always for sale and they lie. So they're more like a consumer disposable product that is used and discarded. Landfill maybe be an appropriate destination."

Phil continued, "The French revolted and chopped its nobility for similar grievances that we in America now face. The nobility were fiscally irresponsible and engaged in unnecessary foreign wars. We revolted and picked off the British from behind trees because of taxation without representation. That's our beef now. The lobbies run the country. Lot's of books and heroes came from those bloody affairs. So assassinating or de-electing some deserving, thieving and lying politicians certainly has an historical base of reference. They auction our rights and future labor to lobbyists that now number about 40,000. They put us in bondage to the servicing of the national debt while they skim more than their fair share. We become a physical chain gang to work off the debt. The preemptive war mongers are my personal targets. Just because Congress agrees on war doesn't make it moral. The war mongers deserve to get strung up. Or should we remove all of them?"

A surprised Gene answered, "Are you having second thoughts? If you want to limit yourself to the warmonger targets, I'm sure there are plenty of other folks who will target the rest. But seriously Phil. How do you organize a rebellion like this? How do you get the message out? How do you inform people of the ultimate goal? How do they know it's not al Qaeda doing the assassinations? How would you write this?"

Phil picked it back up, "You raise a good point. If al Qaeda is blamed then Washington will get what it thrives on—more power, more control. Then that's not the way I want to go. We'll have to make the assassinations look like accidents. Consequently the others in this country who feel like me will be extended a subtle invitation to join. Transitional movements have a life of their own once they get started. It's like the sunshine combines with water and soil to spark life in the dormant seed. It's a fresh wind filling your nostrils while you're overlooking a breathtaking scene of natures handiwork. The plans for the new governmental model comes later. Shoot first. Ask questions and plan later. Boomers and the young have had it with the extravagance, hypocrisy and criminal legislation of elected representatives. Just because 435 members of Congress agree on legislation doesn't mean it's moral. Codifying taste as in the Civil Rights Acts of the 1960s isn't moral and ultimately isn't enforceable. Fuck the politically correct politicians. They piss on our shoes and tell us that it's raining. This could be a chance to give some spice and extra meaning to a life. How many of us have gone along to get along? We quietly obey rules that result in a slow motion death of the spirit and a bankrupting of the economic system. I've read enough history to know we are headed off an economic and social cliff. I don't want to waste time. I know what to value. I know who to remove. I know how to do it and make it look like an accident. It's like my whole life has prepared me for this moment. Our government made murderers of us all. America lost the moral high ground with the Serbian slaughter and then followed it up with the Iraq invasion. Did you know that there were approximately 37,000 jet fighter/bomber sorties in the Serbian campaign? That's barbaric. We were no better than any thug-country in history with those crimes. Why shouldn't Congress and the executive meet the same fate that the ordinary, dead, innocent Iraqi or Serb met? In the Iraqi example, there were two credible surveys, one done by Johns Hopkins University and another conducted by an English group that estimated that over 1,000,000 Iraqis died and approximately 2,500,000 were dislocated from their homes as of the end of 2008. That crime should be punished lest we be guilty also. Silence is complicity and consent."

Gene is a little thrown off by the intensity of Phil. Gene asks, "How much of this is the Negronis, Phil? How much of this talking and planning is a book outline? I don't honestly know if I'm method acting or this is the real me. And I'm not sure about you either. I'm going to have another drink. 'Waiter one more Negroni please'. These waiters are a dying breed. They look and listen and anticipate. Equally important they know when to keep quiet. Sam's business is a metaphor for world commerce. The waiters are mostly European descendants. They're the IT. The kitchen is mostly Asian. They're the manufacturing and labor from the East. China's communism needs America's outsourcing capitalism to work. But America's capitalism needs China's communism to make our democracy work. America fills the slave gap by hiring China's relatively slave-priced workers. But if push comes to shove we need Asia more than Asia needs us. Our democracy fosters a somewhat silent message of better to game the system than to honestly contribute. I've never heard or read of a society that was consumer based that lasted. Rome became consumer based and then declined. China could shut us down economically and as a society without firing one shot. All they would have to do is nationalize our plants and charge more for our outsourcing. Of course our dollar would collapse and China's holding of our treasury notes would suffer but they would still hold the trumps of a work force. We would be forced to pay the higher costs and by extension we would be effectively enslaved to the Chinese. The economic and social lethal fallout from these outsourced jobs is that wealth and our middle class is shipped overseas."

Phil's stream of conscience continued, "The boomers have the motive and opportunity to start the ball rolling. The motive is to dismantle fascist Washington. Bring back states rights. Victor Hugo said,' There is nothing so compelling as an idea who's time has come'. Motivate our boomers to become revolutionary heroes in their waning days. Now that would be a real fountain of youth. Get the gals and guys moving again. Give 'em a goal. Get them out of that shroud of fat and long faces. Hey, put some energy back into your sex life by getting respect from your loved one. Be a hero. Revolution with liberally references to sex would sell books." added Phil with a laugh.

Gene pops off with a smile and high burlesque, "Will the blow jobs come back Phil? Will she be gleefully hopping onto your salivating maw? Would this be a bonus outcome?" Gene continues in a new elevated spirit that came on him naturally, "We could get foundation grants to reward people for information leading to the arrest and conviction of public servants who have committed crimes or impeachable offenses. How could a board of trustees refuse? It's all about trust and public spirited participation."

Phil continues with an acknowledging laugh to Gene's remarks, "O.K., we have motive. Now what's the opportunity look like? The opportunity is the fact every member of Congress is mandated by law to live in their prescribed district of representation. The district would certainly be populated with at least some would-be revolutionary partisans. Legislators walk across busy streets don't they? Let's say it started with just me. I could stalk a representative. Say the rep is at street corner waiting for the signal to change. Suppose I push the rep into car traffic? Say it was a rainy day or at night. Visibility is poor. Nobody would notice me if I did it with care. Many people would flee the scene. They don't want to be questioned by the police. They want to get home. The ones who stayed would be confused and excited. Suppose the worse happens? Someone says that I nudged the rep? So I say someone bumped into me? It would never be first degree manslaughter or murder. Premeditated crimes don't happen that way. No the whole thing would be called an accident. But the fact remained that the member of Congress died or was injured in a public place and in a simple way. Other people would read and think. So that's how it can be done? And soon other accidents are happening across the country. Pretty soon a crowd of our oldies but goodies surround the politician and push him or her into traffic. Now there are no witness' only accomplices. Wouldn't it be wonderful?"

A puzzled-face Gene asks, "How long have you been thinking about this?"

"Just now. The philosophy of a decentralized government I've thought about and favored for a long time. Whether a central government is run by a democracy, a republic, the communists, socialists or kings and emperors they don't work. You can't trust those lying and thieving mandarins, governors, satraps or reps in government. The working plan for removing the thieves I just came up with. Of course my subconscious knew it all along. I just finally allowed it real air time." answered a proud Phil.

"You are astounding." said an amazed Gene tipping his glass in salute.

A puffed up Phil continued, "There's subtle sedition also. Some of our suitable older gals can entrap and exploit a sex scandal. Drugs can be substituted in prescriptions. Make a death or injury look like an attempted robbery. Car mechanics can adjust the brakes so they don't brake. Hey how about impersonating the voice on the navigation system in the car and have them drive into a canyon? Sabotage. Just check your local TV listings. Hell one night of prime time television will give people hundreds of ways to make someone miserable or dead. People are so numbed to misery they can't remember if they saw it on TV or they lived it at home. Hey we could get a hold of a CIA playbook that they use in foreign countries for delicate renditions and removal. Those are easier to obtain than the ones the CIA uses in this country. Our operatives will have to make it look ambiguous. Careful not to expose the real time revolution that's taking place nationally. Give folks an alternative explanation for the removal. Give them an excuse to play dumb but to secretly enjoy."

Gene jumps in after a sip of his Negroni. He can't believe he is getting so enthusiastic about something he just heard about only moments ago. He thinks that this is not normal attorney behavior. But it seems irresistible. But also there's the fact that all attorneys are hired to break laws in a legal way. Why else would I be hired and paid so much more than I'm worth? He thinks to himself, so a law career is merely a first step on the road to caricature of committing a physical murder." Gene says, "How about making use of a cell phone camera. Anytime a representative is spotted, he or she should be followed and photographed. Who are the people he's talking to? Where is she meeting people? Does it look like they are trying to conceal something? Add names and locales with the photographs and then submit it all to a web site that is a clearing house for such information. The website will be advertised on Facebook and Twitter. This alone will have a chilling effect on the daily movements of members of Congress. It could

make many to rethink the whole idea of public employment. Maybe no one has to get killed because of
the enormous pressure of 24/7 scrutiny. Also cross
check the photos, dates and locales against reps log
books. Were they where they were supposed to be?
That's all simple sleuth stuff and it can be fun."

"Great ideas." Phil notices Gene's conversion to
the spirit of the project and is encouraged. Phil continues, "And it's not just older folks. Hell, it's really
the young that should be cleaning up the Congress.
Get something going and I'll bet the kids jump in.
But it should be discreet. I got to work that into the
book also. The jerks of Congress should be taught
the downside of selling lives, rights and things that
don't belong to them. They put the young in bondage
to debt and in harms way from reprisal from countries and people who Congress has wronged in our
name. This whole movement should be run almost
intuitively with a decentralized play book, similar to
all the underground resistance movements. The only
thing our partisans have to do is engage the enemy
and discreetly make life miserable for members of
Congress. But removal has to be done in such a way
as to look like an accident. Then it's harder to prove
as an organized conspiracy. Maybe it ends up that
nobody connects the dots publicly. Or maybe nobody wants to connect the dots publicly. So it looks

like members of Congress are just having a string of bad luck. But nobody cares. Wouldn't that be marvelous?"

"Gene energetically adds, "What are morals or customs against the fact that Congress is a clear danger to our physical and economic health? I would think that younger folks would be eager to join in a revolt. Just look at how young we were in the 1960s war protests. The young will be stuck with the bills. In a way, Congress is drafting young folks now for an economic enslavement later. The kids should burn their republican and democratic ballot suggestions and the tax forms in public like war protesters burned their draft cards. The enemy isn't abroad. It's here. It's in Congress. We always vote for peace but get war. We need to shut down Washington and this motley democracy and go back to the Federalist plans of Washington, Jefferson, Madison and Adams. The right to vote is reserved for peers. People who own property vote on property matters. People who pay taxes vote on matters pertaining to taxes. War is to be determined by a National Referendum. No small groups of politicians in a central government should have that awesome power. Think Truman. Think hat salesman doing nuclear war on a country he probably didn't know existed until after he got into office. He and Congress shouldn't have had that power exclusively. War is the liability of the people. In this one exception it should be a popular vote that decides."

Phil immediately followed and spoke in a sinister way, "I hear that the Fascist bitch's husband has an eye for the ladies. How about some soldier unfolding her legs and squeezing up a sex scandal. Nothing like a diversion in the enemies ranks to help the cause. How about a STD for his trouble. There are plenty of disease cultures available in labs. Our gal could swab him at some opportune moment. And later leak the news that the Speakers husband has the creepy crawlies."

"That's not easy Phil. But suppose a business deal was placed between her legs and Madame Speaker's husband had to do one before he got the other? And what if the business deal blows up because of ru-mored laundered criminal money? There are all sorts of embarrassing scenes that can be staged. And people can be very mean. Just turn those cre-ative destructive juices loose on the politicians. And turn those vicious rumors loose on the internet." re-sponded an equally dark Gene.

Maybe you're right Gene, "Maybe I don't have to swing for the fences? How about Madame Defarge light? Instead of the chop in public, we can also cut and dice to oblivion by many hurts. How many opportunities to mess up a pols life go unused because a older or younger partisan was not thinking in terms of sedition. Bank tellers, drug store clerks, billing people, store help and all the people that engage politicians on a daily basis. If they all were on the lookout for circumstances that could be twisted to make life annoying, to incriminate or worse to the political class then things would progress at an exponential rate. Take photos of bills and checks with cell phones. Submit the documentation to a central website. See if others can find a pattern or evidence that points to crimes or questionable activities. I'm sure we are not alone. And what could be more fun than revolution? Now's the fun time. Planning, setting it up and making strikes before they realize there's a pattern and by that time it's launched and splinter groups join in and voila—critical mass. Now's the exciting time when victory is in doubt but also a victory must be had. This is the sweet spot of a revolution. Because the people who come after us and learn to live in an environment of a decentralized government will in time change and yearn for greater regional relationships and confederacies and toy with the idea of centralizing government again and then inevitably talk empire again in due course and in the end start acting like the assholes we just got rid of." finished Phil in a somewhat disgusted way. Then he finished off his Negroni.

Gene offered this hopeful insight, "We need a barter system. To make sure politics stay local and to
build a stronger social fabric. And to insure there will
be no strong central government. With a barter system one doesn't need seed capital, a business license
or to pay taxes. There you are. You are in business.
You deal with whom you want. You hire the people
you want and no cash gets in the way of your relationships. Couldn't be simpler. Phil do you realize
that women have been using a barter system since
day one. The magic they work with their sexual abili-
ties. And the big magic act of taking some sperm and
presto chango here's junior-take him or leave him.
But if you choose to leave him, please leave cash, lots
of cash. Hey, a fully vested pension for life after only
a nine month pregnancy. But some of those pregnan-
cies should be called infections upon further evalua-
tion of junior. Even after the invention of money the
gals continue to use a barter system. It saves them
the ordeal of actually counting or doing bookkeeping.
And look how far they've gone with just that personal capability and self-indulgence? The male weenies
with P.H.D.s invented Wall Street financial derivative
products. That alchemy created the illusion of a kind
of fabulous wealth. But the simple deal that the ladies offer is more sustainable and has been a proven

wealth creator all along. What a profit margin. Are they are blessed?"

"I bless them." Phil nods and enthusiastically adds.

Phil follows on, "Money is indeed the great tool of distortion."

"Tell me about it", says a somewhat sarcastic Gene. "How about Buffy Warren who spent his whole life accumulating more money than he needed. Now he wants to give it all away mostly to people who don't have his work ethic, mostly to people who shouldn't have been born and all of them shouldn't have had children. Is he commenting on his life? Was it mis-spent? Money explains why we house the criminally insane for life and warehouse other criminals with-out demanding work to offset the costs. In the former the luxury of supporting psychos benefits the prison guard unions and others of the legal system that receive salaries for caring for the incarcerated who don't deserve consideration. Most of those people on death row should have been executed just minutes after the guilty verdict. In just enough time to take them to the curb and put 'em away. In the latter the union philosophy is honored by not having non-union workers doing chores at affordable rates."

Phil agrees and picks it up, "People of all shapes, sizes, races and backgrounds are changed by money. But money alone really doesn't fulfill what people need. They need peace of mind and the security of being in control of their destiny and a fulfillment of a spiritual kind. I'm not talking about religion. I speak of a spiritual oneness with nature. Feeling comfortable in your own skin and where you belong. There has never been more money in circulation than now and I think that consequently the world is more insecure now than ever before. Money doesn't necessarily bring security. It's like we are all playing a game on some clock that is not our time and for some goal that really is not our goal. Money acts like a tectonic shift in the landscape. Either it's too much money or it's too little. It's just one more uncertainty piled on top of mans fragile, uncertain condition. One real negative capability afforded by money is it allows people to be effectively in more than one place at one time. And this has an exponential effect on the humans impact on this relatively small planet. Just think, approximately 7 billion people playing real time creation and destruction with the power that money gives them."

Gene eagerly adds, "A barter system would reduce the anxiety of losing jobs. Use a tool lose and lose your place, is my credo. Barter puts you in more control. Look at the feminine experience. They get their husbands to figuratively do back flips if necessary, even with poor hubby's bad back, to earn a living. They run the house and support their hero and they only have to stay put or maybe mimic Jello for a few moments in bed. Who has the better deal? The women liberation movement was a bad trade for the gals. It got them out of their own kitchen and into a public kitchen. From barter they went to the auction market based on money. That made themselves more likely to be replaced."

Phil anxiously interrupts, "Did you read the recently released figures on sexually transmitted diseases from the Center for Disease Control? It was a study over a five year period. It included over 70,000 participants across all races. The results indicated that 25% of all women between the ages of thirteen and nineteen have a sexually transmitted disease. That's astounding."

"You think there's a corollary between woman's lib and STDs?" asks a somewhat stunned Gene.

Phil answered immediately and with confidence, "Sure there is. So instead of more freedom the gals lost control of their destiny by losing effectively the Good Housekeeping Seal of Approval. Those numbers are frightening. That's 25% of America's upcoming marriage pool that is infected. Those kinds of numbers didn't exist prior to the woman's liberation movement. It's no coincidence that freeing women from their historical role invited all kinds of unintended and unwelcome consequences along with so-called 'freedom'. Betty Friedan was just one typical example of bad advice. Her 'Feminine Mystique' blamed others for the woman's plight. She talked about the 'problem with no name' and the quiet question that married women ask themselves 'Is this all?' She dwelled mostly on negative situations. Surely there were positives. But she didn't speak of those and the trade-offs of freedom."

Gene interrupts, "Interestingly and similarly, Henry David Thoreau in 'Walden' wrote of the husbands condition. He said that '... husbands spend much of their time in quiet desperation.' It would seem that both men and woman were not having fun if Betty and David were to be believed. Maybe the men and women who Friedan and Thoreau wrote about would have also been miserable single? Maybe marriage had nothing to do with two bored people getting married and then staying bored. The remedy is to like yourself and enjoy your own company. Then maybe others will enjoy being around you also?"

Phil picked it up, "That's right. Betty should have looked in the mirror. If you want a better marriage or a better husband then a woman should work on her own skills. She criticized marriages as stifling to women. Did you see some of the other women in her movement — Bella Abzug, Shirley Chisholm, etc? They were not attractive at any level. That had something to do with their rebellion. There isn't anything 'stifling' about supporting your husband like he supports you. And husbands should look in the mirror also and work on their shortcomings. What's good for the goose is good for the gander. Bartering of talents make countries, states, friends and marriages more secure I'll bet if we avoided the woman's liberation movement we would have avoided misogynistic rap music. A key to turning our decaying culture around is to respect women again. The rappers are poster boys for this decadence. They should be horse whipped. Some of those guys talk up murder. How about we feed 'em to the big cats. We could launch our project at feeding time at the zoo. Just before feeding the big cats, we play some rap music. So the association is established. Then on certain days and in certain locales some big cats are released. Any rap music will be followed up by a visit from the large kitties. And there's no killing of endangered cats on penalty of death from the game wardens."

"I like it. But can we get it done? You know there are so many squeamish people." comments a joking Gene.

"Hell, the fucking rap music lovers are not squeamish. They may even think the screams for help are just part of the wall of sound in the music." answers a reassuring Phil with a knowledgeable wink of the eye.

Phil continues in a new direction, "I can't believe the amount of money these fascists are spending. This isn't leadership. It's like Rome's Bread and Circus policies shortly before it was over run by the Huns, Goths, Gauls. By contrast the Afghans mostly barter. They kicked out Alexander The Great, Genghis Khan, the British Empire, the Soviet Union and now NATO and the U.S.. The implied question posed by a democratic army versus an army made up of members who barter is 'Do you want to die for money and somebody's business model or die for your own values?' Greece's democracy and the Soviet Union's communist governments are both gone. But Afghanistan's largely barter society prevails. We want the Afghans to adopt democracy? Actually we should study and adopt their social philosophy of a barter system if we want to prevail."

Gene responds, "I'm skeptical. Is it really only a choice of barter or punching a time clock?"

Phil replies, "The clock belongs to another. The profits go to another. So, why work and die for another. If you die, it's not really you that died, it's really a property loss by another. Is that the way you want to end up? That's the choice that seem to be presenting itself. You can try to squirm a different explanation or reason but I think in the end it will boil down to that. Of course the members of Congress would add that you owe your life and fruits of your labor to the other citizens. To which I would say, 'No'."

Gene counseled, "Shouldn't we cool off Phil? We're not doing badly at all. Play the game for a few more years. The world markets are keeping an eye on our liberal legislation and how it effects our dollar. The foreign exchange markets can dry up funds. That will put a damper on our greedy legislators. Remember, we are a debtor nation that depends on the 'kindness of strangers' to quote Blance Du Bois."

Phil piked up on the movie quote. He said, "Did Vivien Leigh have a nose job? I saw her in 'Sidewalks of London' with Charles Laughton and Rex Harrison some time ago. It was most enjoyable. It was a much earlier movie than 'Streetcar Named Desire'. I swear her nose was longer. Do you think it was bobbed?"

Gene was eager for a new direction in conversation. He said, "I don't know. But Olivier couldn't handle his wife's triumph in 'Gone With The Wind'. The vintage footage at the Academy Awards showed an uncomfortable man. Was he a homosexual?"

"Who knows. Actors don't seem comfortable with themselves most of the time. That's why they act." said a philosophical Phil. "In the beginning there was truth. Then came lies. Then came politics. Then came acting. They hybridized themselves in Reagan. But another actor/politician was Jack Kennedy. Reagan actually had a job acting. Kennedy never had an acting job per se but became a politician because he could act. His father was the impresario. Remember RKO? K was for Kennedy. That studio turned out some good movies. Astaire and Rogers collaborations, Citizen Cane and lots more."

"Hollywood and Congress are enclaves of fantasy. Both are sustained by the gullible." Gene observed.

Phil loved to talk about movies and movie trivia. They were a big part of his growing up. He spoke with new energy, "Movies have always interested me but only in a rather narrow time period. Roughly from the 1930s to approximately the late 50s. There are exceptions. The movie houses would have a new feature every two weeks. That lasted until Congress separated production from distribution through a divestiture decree against Paramount in 1945. That was the beginning of the end of fresh, daring dramas featuring a rich, experienced repertory company and great directors. What followed over time was overpaid, independent actors, ad hoc directors and formula movies and their many sequels. The movie business went from art run as a business to a business with some art if you could find it. There was a time in Hollywood. Many say that the golden year was 1939. Gone With The Wind, Wizard Of Oz, Stagecoach, Wuthering Heights, The Hunchback Of Notre Dame and many more were produced. Classic stories that were well directed and acted by real people. By real people, I mean actors who had experiences in the real, harsh world of the depression and the rich world that preceded it. It all was on their faces. The camera and the lighting picked it all out. They drew on those experiences. That's where their value added came from. Today our actors faces and voices don't reflect that depth of those kinds of life experiences. They simply were not exposed to it. Movies are art. It can be great art. If one wants to communicate an idea or message, a great movie is a good way to influence." commented Phil.

Phil segued, "That reminds me. The plains Indians wouldn't let their pictures be taken because they
feared the camera would snatch their souls. They instinctively made that very sophisticated point. Years
later they posed and were photographed in shows like
Buffalo Bill's Wild West without protest. He was the
asshole who earned his 'Buffalo Bill" nickname by
slaughtering 4860 of the gentle beasts in an eighteen
month period. But by then all the Indians were all
on reservations. Sad. They knew they had lost their
souls. I wonder if Irving Berlin knew about Buffalo
Bill and the history of Indians in America? His rous-
ing song, 'There's No Business Like Show Business'
from 'Annie Get Your Gun' somewhat disconnects
from the realities of Buffalo Bill and the Indians in
that movie. Although it works marvelously as entertainment."

Gene jumps in, "That line 'show people smile when
they are low' was most accurate. I think Lorenz Hart
of Rodgers and Hart wrote some of the best lyrics
ever. Songs like 'Where Or When, Lover, Bewitched,
I Could Write a Book'. Of course they wouldn't have
worked so well without Rodgers music. But he was
a poet. He must have been a fragile and vulnerable
man with that kind of perception and sensitivity."

Phil nods in agreement and says, "I think he's

great also. Cole Porter was tops too. 'Begin the Beguine, Your The Top, Night and Day, Got You Under My Skin.' Sinatra agreed with our choices. Those songs were included in most Sinatra performances. Sinatra treated his voice like a musical instrument. He has been quoted, ' I was impressed with Tommy Dorsey's control of the trombones sound and I wanted to duplicate that control on my own voice'. He together with arranger and orchestra leader Nelson Riddle and the great song writers performed the American song book in an unsurpassed way. Sinatra hit the notes, according to Riddle. Riddle commented on Dean Martin's singing by saying that he sang between the notes. But it worked for Dino." said Phil.

"I wish I could listen to them right now and there was a dance floor." agreed Gene in a dreamy and romantic way.

"That's entertainment. That will get your blood moving and your spirit soaring. After a fencing tournament on the road, I'll have dinner and a couple of drinks and then go back to the room to come down off the highs. I surf the channels looking for old movies. What crap is being shown. It's mean spirited and mostly violent with soft porn. Kids have access to this garbage? Woe is us. The place is filling up. Want some espresso and a salmbocca?" asked Phil.

"Sounds good." Gene waves to the waiter. "What did you think of the hermaphrodite Michael Jackson's dancing?"

"He is more an exhibitionist of aerobics than dancing. Someone said he picked up where Astaire and Kelly left off and took dancing to a new better level. I don't think so. Astaire and Kelly accommodated partners gracefully while this freak just amused himself. He didn't want nor do I think he could mentally handle a female partner. Eleanor Powell, Cyd Charisse or Rita Hayworth with Kelly or Astaire, that's the best. That's a dancing exponential." Phil commented with much nostalgia.

Gene asks, "What's most important? The director, actor or screen play?"

"The director, followed by the screen play and then the actor." a sure Phil replied.

"The director is important. But how can a good screenplay and good directing be believable and entertaining without credible actors? You said yourself it's either on the actors face or don't bother to stay seated in the theater." Gene rhetorically answers.

"Good point. The Greeks wore masks of comedy

or tragedy and relied a great deal on the chorus to recite and bring the story alive. It doesn't look like directing was much of a chore except in a logistical way. It seems that the writer of the play was the guy. Actors and directors came later as focal points it looks like. They made an indifferent story interesting and entertaining by their value added. But the movie goes over the top when the director and the capable actor combine to develop and present a great script." An engaged Phil says with a sense of discovery in his voice.

Gene picks it back up, "Only the story lasts. Actors and directors come and go. It's like metaphysics, it endures while the components wear out. Most are more interested in the actors rather than the story. A passage in Mac Beth is quite wonderful and apropos. It goes,' Life is a walking shadow, a poor player that struts and frets his hour upon the stage and is heard no more, it is a tale told by an idiot, full of sound and fury and signifying nothing.' A quick test for any person you might be interested in would be to watch TV and see what she watches and what she mutes if she mutes anything. The mute button on a TV remote control is a subtle honest test."

"To your health, to mute buttons and to Shakespeare's observation." Phil toasts Gene and they touch glasses a little more forcibly as the drinks take effect." Speaking of 'poor players who strut and fret', look who just came in. The former mayor who's name should be 'Untitled' because... well just look at that face. And our present hag to fags and nanny to all, Mayor Gayvin Nuisance and the head of Muni, Rex Karz. They must not have taken a Muni bus to get here because we would have seen and heard a crash through the front door with one or two pedestrians on the buses windshield. Those drivers will do anything to get some potato chips from the bar. Have you seen some of them? They need a wheelchair ramp to get into the drivers seat. Next they will drive the bus over the driver and pull him and his modular driving pod up into the cab. The Muni Union is very powerful. If 'Untitled' and the Muni Union are any indications, maybe we are close to a bottom in San Francisco culture and also the nations culture by extension. But that also indicates an economic collapse is not far behind. A plunging economic environment is the only sure fire way to get constructive change. The obese canary in America's cultural mine will then become fit. Supposedly, two thirds of the U.S. population is obese. An economic collapse will certainly cinch up the belt. That's a positive to come from calamity."

Gene asks in an affected air of seriousness, "Why

don't you go over and ask the mayors, 'Have we hit
bottom yet?' Let's tell' em we thought the bottom was
'Untitled' until Nuisance showed up. Did you see
the proposal by the Board of Supervisors. It's in the
paper today. They want to construct wind turbines
throughout the city to generate electricity."

"What's next?" asks an incredulous Phil. He then
answers his own question, "How about everyone has
to wear propeller beanies to feed back into the electric
grid. This includes tourists who have to rent beanies
while they stay in SF. I have a better idea. How about
we just compost Nusiance and the Board of Stupidvi-
sors for methane gas? That will make them good for
something. Look Silver is joining them. She's looking
at us while talking to them. And now they are all
looking at us. Gayvin Nuisance is looking at me like
I'm somewhat familiar.

Gene asks, "Have you met Nuisance?"

Phil answers with a reflective sound in his voice,
"No. I'm pretty sure not. But I was close friends with
his late uncle. Rick was a great guy. He drank and
smoked to much and that's what did him in. But
what a raconteur. Maybe the mayor knows of me?"

Gene says with some intensity, "That's possible.

I get the feeling he may come over by the look of his body language and Silver's story."

Phil answered, "If only Fascista-Cana were here. Then Nuisance would have his two mommies by his side. I can't believe this guy launched a gubernatorial campaign. He's finding out fast that outside of the homosexual community and the teen groupies he really has no credibility. His rival in the democratic party has out raised him in money by about ten to one. And he's ahead of Nuisance by 20 points in the polls even with San Francisco voters."

Gene says, "The guy's an empty suit. He started by running a geeky campaign that was launched on Twitter or Facebook."

Phil responds, "We will make use of those web sites also when we launch our revolution and sedition campaign. Like any tool it can do good or it can do damage. If the morons want to Twitter by the hundreds of thousands on rumors of a center fold beaver shot of a spread eagle Jennifer Aniston appearing in OK! or 'People' magazine, let them."

Gene roars with laughter and answers, "Jennifer Aniston beaver shot'? Where do you get this stuff? Nuisance is no leader. He just uses a dim light to show the way to a lower cultural level. Those homo-sexual marriages that he authorized got Shrub elect-ed. I think many in the Democratic party are afraid he's the type who doesn't learn from mistakes but just goes on to make greater ones. I predict he will go into political oblivion."

Phil agrees and answers, "If we were leaving I'd go to their table and indeed ask them when the City was going to hit bottom? But I don't want to pressure Darius any further."

Gene counseled, "Yeah, let's not put anymore pressure on poor Darius."

"How about we ask some of the folks who respond-ed favorably to my loud talk about killing members of Congress to take our part?" Phil said half in fun, half seriously.

Gene asked a serious question, "I wonder how many times this kind of public rebuke has happened to Silver? How many times has she been verbally abused in a public place? She got very angry and red in the face. It looked like she was caught off guard and unprepared. It doesn't look like this happened before. Does she suspect something like 'the lesson of the sombrero'?"

"What is the sombrero lesson?" asked Phil who's face showed an ignorance of the term.

"Well, when the defenders of the Alamo saw a sombrero on the horizon coming from Mexico, they immediately suspected that there were many more behind that one. Sadly, they were correct. The rest is history. Our behavior today toward Silver could signal to her that there are others like us out there. She will never forget this episode. I wouldn't be surprised if she announces her retirement from the Senate in the not-to-distant future." said an analytical Gene.

A supportive Phil said, "At some point these carpetbaggers must suspect their governmental double dealing will end. The music will stop at some point. And then the people in office will get the full force of anger and revenge from the people. That time is close. All chaotic changes are preceded by an economic meltdown that does not have a recovery. This may be that meltdown. This meltdown may not have a recovery. It has happened before. Only the most greedy and the ones who stay too long gorging at the public trough get wiped out. Silver may suspect the beginning of the end. Her reaction signals vulnerability. But don't count on a retirement. Remember she's a Zionist and they never give anything back. Plus they would become more vulnerable to a popular

anti Zionist and anti-Israel movement in this country if they were not in control to manage a response.
Actually I think the Zionists in Congress are more
determined now than ever before to remain in power
and extend their control. They are somewhat running scared. They see the form of the backlash and
they don't want to be split up. So they intensify their
efforts which only brings more backlash. They have
made the same type of mistakes in the past. They
make themselves effectively stupid because of their
arrogance and greed and refusing to accept moderation. They are an all or none race in a subtle—difference world. That's one of the reasons there are so few
left in the world."

Gene predicts, "When the checks don't cash,
that's when the morons who are sipping their brews
while watching professional sports will get off the
couch. Then they'll head out into the streets to see
what can be done."

Something changes Phil's focus. He turns the
conversation into another direction. He says, "Coming over here today, I run into a traffic jam behind
an ambulance. The ambulance is double-parked
on Bush Street on a fairly steep incline in the right
lane. It's a one way street. I think it was around Polk
Street. I was close to the ambulance. The lights were

flickering. The air was filled with diesel smoke as the noisy engine idled on without purpose. A loud voice on the radio in the ambulance was trying to get a response from the paramedics but they had their hands full in the rear of the truck. Two paramedics looked like they were delivering an older woman to her home. She's on this high gurney. Really too high to be stable. One paramedic is a black dude who's at least 6'3" and the other is an Asian woman no bigger than 4'11". Added up and divided by two they met the height requirements of San Francisco's all are equal policies. S.F.'s policies rely on creative math to make them work. The tall guy is standing at the head of the patient. The shorter medic is at the foot of the patient. Add in the steep incline of Bush Street and you have roughly a four foot drop from dude to Asian, head to head. The short gal is trying to control the foot of the gurney. The feet of the lady are big and almost touching the face of the short medic. I don't know if the paramedics speak English because no one is talking. Only abrupt gestures are given. Something drops from the gurney. The short medic lets go of her end to pick it up. She moves quickly and the gurney starts to roll down the hill. The old lady screams and clutches the rig. The tall guy just barely grabs the gurney because he was waving and scoping out some chicks legs in a slow moving car driving by. He tries to reassure the patient while giving his assistant a dirty look. They finally start moving the gurney toward the sidewalk. The old ladies flat is atop a steep outside staircase. At that time the traffic breaks free and a car drives slowly by the gurney. The cars windshield washers are being used and the water mists the old lady who screams, ' It's raining'. I would have like to have stayed and see the assault on the staircase. It would be akin to the troops on Omaha Beach scaling the heights of Normandy Beach. Only instead of the troops it would be only 2 paramedics. And instead of the Nazis it would only be gravity and the staircase as the enemy. I don't think the black dude or the Asian fully grasped their physical world adversaries. They didn't have to when applying for their San Francisco jobs. But I had to go. I wonder what happened?" Phil could hardly contain his deep laughing.

"They still may be there. Why not drive back to see?" says an entertained Gene who's chuckling.

While the two men were talking intensely, they didn't notice a modestly dressed man in good shape confidently walk to the table. He said, "Hi. I don't want to disturb you gentlemen. But I sat over there and have heard much of your intriguing conversation. It makes me feel 40 years younger. Time and pressure makes us somewhat cowardly. And we forget how vigor and confidence brought on by an important mission in life suits us well because it makes us stretch. My name is Bill Duesenberg."

"Hi Bill. I'm Gene Ray and this is Phil Di Caesari. I didn't realize we were talking so loud. But we are having fun. Sit down. Have a drink. Waiter. What will you have, we're buying?" Both Phil and Gene were struck with the self assured demeanor of Bill.

"Just a glass of white wine please. Thanks. Like I said it acts like an elixir to hear of the prospects of personally having a hand in giving congressional representatives what they have long deserved. What ever form it may take. From a simple car accident to one clean shot from a high building." said Bill in an astounding disconnect from what one might think this man would talk about. Phil thought, maybe this guy had the genes or buried memories of some long ago knight who traveled his country bringing justice to roving thugs and hooligans.

Phil looks at Gene and Gene looks back. They both have the same thought. Duesenberg thinks the conversation about assassinations is real. Phil doesn't address that issue and changes the subject, "Any relation to the famous car builders of Indiana, the Duesenberg brothers?"

"Yes, I'm related to them. But I think they started in Des Moines, Iowa" replied Bill in a dismissive way. It was obvious that Bill had more important questions or ideas to discuss. He wanted to talk about assassinations!

"That 1935 Duesenberg Model SJ LA Grand Dual-Cowl Phaeton was the 'Duesy'. Women in diaphanous gowns with art deco jewelry. Architecture like the Chrysler and the Empire State Buildings in New York City, gentlemen accessories by Tiffany and Cartier, music by Cole Porter and the Gershwins, dancing to Eddy Duchin's orchestra at Central Park Casino, that was an American high point in style. Are you retired?" asked Phil who didn't yet know what he was going to do about clarifying his conversation to Bill. He kind of liked the idea of influencing people. And this quick response by the public made Phil feel important and he didn't want to through it away too quickly.

"I taught ancient history and literature at the University in Champagne/Urbana, Illinois. I'm visiting San Francisco with my wife who is shopping. There's just so much a guy can take when shopping. So I took a break." Bill spoke crisply and looked at the two men directly and intensely.

"I know. For women it's like the first time they have ever gone shopping every time they go. Can you imagine if they turned that kind of enthusiasm and spirit of discovery into studying quantum physics?" said an entertaining Gene. Gene was also wondering how Phil was going to handle the confusion on Bill's part? Or should he speak up?

Phil reenters with an on message statement, "Revolutions. It's all there in the history books. Want to know the future look at the past."

"Yep. But I never read about a revolution being led by the older folks. Of course history repeats but isn't bound to an exact replica." answered Bill in a way that sounded like he would like to be part of the older folks doing a new variation on old revolutionary movements.

Phil remembers an important part of his life. He doesn't want to forget the question. Also it gives him more time in the role of a bona fide charismatic leader. He promises himself he will clue in Duesenberg shortly. But now he asks, "Did you know a horseman by the name of Richard Brooks who lived in Champagne some 30 years ago?"

Bill after a pause for recollection, answered, "No.

Were you a horseman?"

"Yep. I lost my last horse in 2005. I sure miss him and all the other pets I've had. One thing good about death. I'm going to find out where all my pets went. But Brooks was a judge at a show in Monterrey when my wife and I showed our gelding Castle Star Reporter in 1978. We swept all the classes he was entered." Phil said in a heavy moment of nostalgia. It was like the days he spent with his horses were the best days.

Bill jumped in because he was constrained by time and also because he wanted to talk more revolution. "I have to meet my wife shortly. The trouble with our politicians and by extension our voters is that there are no priorities. We vote money we can't afford to any project that comes along. It's like Congress is god and prints money and through that alchemy grants every wish to every lobby. Nobody says 'No' because they wont get elected. Well even god has to take away for every thing he gives. It's a zero sum planet. I told my students that you can philosophize and use rhetorical arguments all you want but if the metaphysics of the scheme of things is ignored you will fail to the extent that you don't pay respect to natural laws. One example is the wonder drugs of antibiotics. That's one big reason why we are over-populated. If we are going to play by gods rules then if someone receives antibiotics then he or she has to use an equal amount of contraceptives. The ratio and proportions can be worked out but I don't hear of anyone talking about that. Any way I've got to go. I'm in the phone book if you need a contact in the mid west. Thanks guys and good luck. Do you want me to spill water on those pols over there? I've read about that Senator Silver. She's a fuckin' phony. Pardon my language. But I feel comfortable with you both."

"Bill, you said, '..if the metaphysics of the scheme is ignored it will fail..' Did you hear Phil say much the same thing about '... ignoring real time metaphysics' in relation to passing laws that are not sustainable' some time ago? Asked Gene with much curiosity in his voice.

"No I didn't hear anything really till the '..let's kill members of congress' outburst." Bill said with a curious smile and a laugh.

"I asked because that's the same reason Phil gave for failing legislation and regulations that Congress regularly churns out. i.e. it ignores the realities of metaphysics or natural law." said Gene directly with more than just some amazement.

"I'll be darned." said a startled Bill. "That is a co-incidence. Then again it's not really, it's a fact that keeps coming up regularly nowadays but no one wants to pay attention to it, save a few. One thing more. It's later than a lot of people think."

"What do you mean?" asks an intent Phil.

"Remember all the money I said we're printing?" asked Bill.

"Yeah. We know. But what about it?" asked Gene.

"Well the Chinese and speculators around the world are buying hard commodities like oil, copper and aluminum with it. They aren't stupid. They gather we show no respect for creditors so they cash our play money in on hard assets. The problem for us is that our recovery depends on reasonably priced commodities. But those commodities are being bid up. That sets up a vicious cycle for us. The more money we print to spend our way out of the recession the more commodities go up. We make progress but the commodities are moving faster than our progress, so fast that the recovery might be stalled. It won't be pretty. It could cause a revolution if peoples checks don't cash. It's the long awaited day of reckoning for America's democracy. Something like what Rome went through in its decline. Well I got to hop. You sure you don't want me to spill anything on Silver when I leave?"

"No thanks Bill. But we may call on you to be a field marshal in the mid west." says Gene who is somewhat shocked by Bill's prognosis.

Phil finally fesses up, "Bill, that outburst of mine 'Let's Kill Members Of Congress' was an inspirational moment for me. I finally got the title I'd been struggling to find. It's about the title for a new book I'm writing. I became aware of my screaming and then lowered my voice. I have changed the title into 'Who Is Killing Members Of Congress?'. It had to do with the book title, Bill. I was not calling for the slaughter of Congress. I apologize. I'm embarrassed. Do I make myself clear?"

Bill looks at Phil and Gene. Now he's embarrassed. He's lost for a response. Many thoughts flood his mind. What do these guys think of me? Boy do I look and sound like a shut-in. But then he composes himself and says with conviction, "Fiction today. Fact tomorrow". He shakes hands with both men and then leaves.

"Wow. Quite a guy. There's got to be a lot out there somewhat like Bill. But he's one of a kind. But with just a little encouragement more people would step forward. The old saying that goes something like, 'Times make the man or a man for the times?' He's very impressive. I loved his self assured and crisp way of speaking. He had a knowledge of history which was coupled with a good way of speaking. I could talk to him all day." observes an excited Phil.

"I wonder what his wife is like? She must be somewhat like him. Of course you never know, but teachers talk and are empathetic so she probably has knowledge of her husbands beliefs. She probably agrees." Gene guessed.

Gene opens a new subject for conversation. "Roman Polanski is back in the news. He's in Switzerland fighting extradition to the U.S. There is an outstanding warrant for his arrest on a morals charge. It date backs some twenty or thirty years ago. He drugged a thirteen year old and then had sex with her. He pleaded guilty but jumped bail and fled the country."

Phil added, "He wrote 'Chinatown'. Jack Nicholson, Faye Dunaway and John Huston were in it. It's based on the draining of Owens Valley and the bring-

ing of water to what was to become the greater Los
Angeles sprawl. It tells how the money was made by
buying up huge tracks of dry land that would blos-
som soon with piped Owens Valley water and drive
up land prices. He also wrote 'Rosemary's Baby'. It's
about the devil in the form of an animal impregnating
a hapless white girl. Maybe it's a metaphor for what
happens to white girls in Hollywood? He's weird."

"Yeah. There's a sub plot which has Huston having a child with his young teenage daughter. Polanski wrote the script while in France or London. I guess
he wanted to minimize his crime by putting Huston's
incest pregnancy up on the screen. Polanski got an
Academy Award for his efforts. The Hollywood Jew
tribe sticks together." Gene adds.

"Speaking of Hollywood and morals, Joseph Mc-
Carthy's House Un-American Committee held hearings. That turned into largely a Jewish communist
affair. The 'black lists' followed. McCarthy had a
point. Communist propaganda and its preaching of
an overthrow of our government. Those subversive
movies were shown across the country. It would be
similar to our national distribution of rapper record-
ings that talk up crime and women abuse. It offends
many. But no one is holding hearings. But McCarthy
held hearings. He just asked questions. It's not his

fault that the answers all pointed to Jewish Communists as the culprits who were probably engaged in
an act of coordinated sedition." observed Phil.

Phil continued, "Went to my first opera the other
night with an old friend. Saw Puccini's Il Trittico. Had
box seats, three hundred per seat. It was a wonderful experience."

"I haven't seen an opera." said Gene in an almost
ashamed way.

"I never realized how the acting ability of the sing-
ers played such an important part. The box seats let
you really zero in on the faces. I was engaged even
without the small binoculars. Then the voices took
over. Wow. They acted well and sang wonderfully.
The music was beautifully arranged and conducted
by an energetic leader. I had a birds eye view of the
orchestra pit. That was an unexpected bonus. I'm
going to get season tickets from now on." said an
excited Phil.

"I think an opera binocular is called a lorgnette.
Where did you go after wards?" asked a very interested Gene.

"It was a matinee on Sunday. It started at two

and ended about four-thirty. We went to a restaurant nearby called Jardins. I had been there before. The prices were still very high but the quality of food, drinks and service went down." said Phil in a downbeat way.

"So Puccini's hundred year old opera was served up better than the groceries? Does that prove that we don't live by bread alone?" Gene asked, trying to jam philosophy into a simple statement.

"I guess so. I'm still thinking and talking about the performance. But I want to forget the dinner. I know I'm defying the odds but any good news in the Chronicle today?" asked Phil in a childlike way.

"Actually there is. Four dams on the Klamath are going to be razed starting in 2020. A three hundred mile stretch of the river which was a prime salmon run will be returned to the remarkable fish. It had been shut down by the dams for the past one hundred years. It decimated the salmon stocks. But last years collapse of the salmon season got all the players in the ten year old negotiations on the same page and it got done. The dams belong to PacificCorp. That's a Buffy Warren company. He's in everything where a buck is to be made. The guy is a freak of nature." Gene stated.

"To be more accurate, he's a freak of money. There's a difference. Money per se does not exist in nature. Money created Buffy. He's the result of alchemy. He's the pulsating, munching, walking and talking 'bidness-man'. What a bore." noted Phil.

Gene has a flash, "It's funny with people like Buffy Warren. They go so far in one direction that they become a cartoon of a money making business man. At some point he maybe gets bored or self conscious about his wealth and decides to start a new life. But what kind of life will he start over with? The only place that is left open is to go in the direction that he's avoided up until now. He becomes an activist for the poor wherever they may live. I.E. he takes up the plight of the starving Africans with the guidance of the Gates Foundation."

Phil counters, "That's funny because he meets Oprah on her circuitous journey from a black, female activist to a cartoon of a business woman with her over-dressing and the multiple enterprises of self promotion."

Gene nods and asks," Both were driven by money. I wonder what kind of people they would be without money?

Phil thinks a bit and says, "How about Buffy being a bean counter and Oprah being a bean eater?

Gene wasn't impressed. He asks, "Who did you go to the opera with?"

"He's a long time friend from the time I made markets and traded on the floor of the exchange. He made markets also. He did very well and he's a good guy. He had these multiple indicators that he followed to track market turns in direction. We'd pull his chain and say, 'Hey Al, what do your 341 indicators say now?'. That would imply that by the time he analyzed all the data he would have missed the time of the crucial change in direction." Phil said laughingly.

"Do you miss the action on the floor?" asked Gene who sensed some nostalgia in Phil when he spoke of his past career.

"When I first went down there in the late seventies it was great. You lived a life each day. Laugh and scream and go home hoarse and tired but anticipating coming back for more action the next day. I was hooked on volatility. There was good money to be made if you managed risk. If you didn't, you could lose more money faster than a sour streak at a

Las Vegas crap table. But then in the early eighties, Chicago offered some new financial derivative products that were designed to track a broad market index direction. That new product took business away from us. Because we were involved with single stock options which required a smaller target to hit. Chicago's product only required someone get the general markets direction accurately to cash in. So you can see the difference. Our derivative products were heavily regulated. Unlike the junk that was at the bottom of the recent financial meltdown. Over time our franchise become less lucrative and eventually the floor closed three or four years ago." said Phil with some regret.

"It sure sounded like fun. Nothing that lucrative and also enjoyable can possibly last too long. I guess it was only a matter of time before Wall Street took financial derivative products to the next level by making it a cartoon of a happy, joy giving, money machine even if it required stomping on the concept of fair play and ultimately wrecking the financial system." said a savvy Gene.

Phil was pleased that his friend picked up the esoteric facts of his business so quickly and answered, "You got that right. 'Derivative financial products', it does indeed hint at other words for gambling. That thought crossed Wall Street's mind also. That's why the attorneys and lawmakers excluded these financial products from individual state gaming laws. That was expressly put into The Futures Modernization Act of 2000. That Act made universal the Enron loophole which lifted position limits on commodity speculation. That immediately drove up the prices of basic materials. It also cleared the way for mortgage backed securities and collateral debt obligations to be traded without, I repeat, without government regulation or oversight. That's better than a 'get out of jail pass' because no one was going to go to jail in the first place no matter what happened. These products were effectively proprietary gambling chips issued by Wall Street's investment bankers. They invented them, made markets in them and lied about their credit worthiness to buyers around the world. But none of this would or could have happened without the complicity of our government. Laws had to be repealed. New laws had to be passed prohibiting regulation. They needed Congress. Al told me that in the past four or five years Wall Street gave approximately six billion dollars to key members of Congress that controlled and voted on The Streets products. No one will serve time because all the heretofore breaking of rules were repealed so there were no laws broken. It was legal. That's pretty rotten. These people in Congress are supposed to be the gate keepers and watch out for the commonwealth. My ass. They were in on the scheme. They enabled it. You can't have laws that ignore fair play and morality. You know, treat others as you would like to be treated. If it doesn't. Then feel free to take matters into your own hands for the purpose of self defense." said an agitated and determined Phil.

"Do you think anyone will put the pieces together?" asked Gene.

"It wont matter. Because they stole legally. It's oxymoron time in America. It's George Orwell's 1984 'doublespeak'. So instead of fraud and embezzlement charges, the bonus babies biggest challenge will be to pay the least taxes. We have to do something about members of Congress before their next step to caricature involves even more destructive steps. Voting doesn't get things changed. We need more persuasive and permanent fixes for the thieving members of Congress," Phil said with determination.

"Goldman Sachs looks more of danger and threat to Americas future than al-Qaeda." stated an insightful Gene. "Speaking of al-Qaeda, our government just approved foreign aid to Pakistan in the amount of $1.5 billion per year for 5 years. It's for a public relations effort to make the U.S. presence in that region more understandable and us more likeable. In reality. I think it's a bribe to Pakistan's government so they'll continue to let us use our drones in pursuit of the Taliban and al-Qaeda on Pakistani soil. The money is to mitigate the political heat they get when our drones also kill innocent Pakistanis. We have fuckin' morons running our government and armed forces. We have 60,000 or so troops in Afghanistan. That's half of NATO's total. The commanding general just asked for an additional 40,000. Here's some prospective of the mismatch of our manpower versus the Taliban. The New York City police department is approximately 40,000 and that's to police city dwellers who cooperate and want peace. We're losing and it will only get worse."

"What about the air power back ups?" asked Phil.

"Taken as a whole, the net effect of air power is to drive the normal Afghan into resenting the U.S. presence because of the collateral loss of life and property damage. Those morons at the Pentagon had the "shock and awe" plans perfectly planned on paper. But the reality is you are dealing with people and people always make mistakes. But when you are dealing with laser guided 1000 pound bombs your mistakes stand out and are irreversible." complained Gene.

"Are you going to the reunion next week?" asked
Phil.

"Yeah. It's at Castagnolas. The food is OK and they
have a small private bar available. If it weren't for the
name tags I wouldn't recognize at least half. But as
soon as I reacquaint, those memories flood back and
with some it's like we just stepped out of some room
moments ago and now we pick up the conversation
where we left off. Of course the topics are different
but the friendly comfortable conversation is what's
familiar and enjoyable. We've lost two classmates in
the past year. Paul Hogan died of emphysema and
Jack Conneely had a heart attack. They were wonderful. Time has rolled by. But actually the relationship
defied time. There really isn't time without change.
And since the relationship didn't change, time really
didn't enter into it. Of course the faces had changed
but the same guys were still in there. We had a great
class. The Class of 1961. There were turbulent times
in San Francisco. The talk was about the Summer of
Love in 1967 but love was not the whole story, The
drugs and unhealthy life styles more than offset the
free love escapades and the good music. Was it all
worth it? Probably not. But people only learn by mistakes. So pushing the envelope of experiences was
unavoidable. Best things to come out of those years
was the environmental movement and the establish-

ment of an enduring anti-war philosophy. They made
our school co-ed some 5 or six years ago. I wonder
what difference that makes to education? One thing
it would do, it would establish man/woman relations
in all their many forms earlier." spoke Gene reflec-
tively.

Phil stated energetically, "I like the ladies. Would
I like them more or less had I gone to school with
them? Probably 'like' is the wrong question. Would I
feel more comfortable would be a better test or comparison? I guess I would have felt more comfortable
sooner with a coed exposure because I was raised an
only child."

Gene jumps in and quotes Phil, "... coed exposure...' uh? You can't avoid double *entendres*."

A smiling Phil answers, "I'm a natural poet. I went
to one of those reunion lunches last year. It was fun.
No PC, no affectations to speak of just easy, friendly
talk. Remember Jung? He was popping off on how
his people now had what was left of San Francisco in escrow. I told him I was glad he was doing so
well. But I wasn't happy about his relatives good for-
tune because I never met them. So I told him that I
didn't want to fret about my future. Living with all
those Chinese would be dangerous. Particularly driv-

ing with them daily. So I challenged Jung to play Moriarity eighteen holes for Jung and his families holdings in the city. I would throw my holdings and my families holdings in. Winner take all. Moriarity said that would be a lot of pressure. But I told Mike not to worry. I'd have a sniper in the tall cypress on the eighteenth if we needed a back up. Then there was Dr. McGinty who was not mindful of the beer bottle in his hand while he's telling the guys he was a urologist. Someone exaggerated a move to unzip and then McGinty caught on. The lunch flew by. Oh yeah, Alioto showed up."

Gene interrupts, "Let me guess. One of his children is running for public office?"

Phil fires back, "You're half right. Actually two of his children are running for office. He's wearing this suit that must have cost him three grand. I asked him if I could borrow it? He said he would rent it to me. He asked if I wanted the shoes also? We had a good laugh."

"Gene laughed and he continued, "I went to the yearly cross town basketball game against Sacred Heart some years ago with Gary Gianinni. You missed it. We were seated near the band. Just watching the members of the band was a kick. Was it fun. There was a small cute girl with her short skirt playing a trombone. If the slide was extended and she stood along side it, the instrument would be as tall as her. There was one big guy playing the flute. The guy on drums was lost in a Gene Krupa-like pounding ecstasy. There was a tuba player who punctuated, a clarinet guy who had a deliberate and reserved Benny Goodman posture that didn't come naturally. And a couple of Asian girl violin players who were very studious but were having a ball. And there was this little guy playing the base sax. When he wasn't standing he had to sit on something extra to keep the saxophone off of the ground. A huge gal dwarfed her french horn so it looked like the instrument was a mere bauble that might have been on her necklace. Two guys on trumpet who looked and sounded like they were dueling. Consequently the horns were menacingly thrust at each other and the boys raced into the notes and alternatively blew harder than required leaving behind the rest of the band. The smiling, sweating and admonishing band leader had as much control as an engineer on a runaway locomotive. But it all worked because of the energy of enthusiasm. The scripted music ranged from the theme song of 'Mission Impossible' when there was a turnover from S.I. to S.H. to the ' Terminators' menacing low throbbing refrain when S.I. was coming down court to its basket. The intensity of the ball players was truly inspirational. Outside of the NBA the players must still dribble the ball when they walk or run. That's the original basketball protocol. There's no giant strides and then crashing like a wrecking ball into the opponents under the basket in high school or college basketball. Amateur events are the best way to the enjoy the sports."

"Sorry I missed it. When is it again?" asked an anxious Phil.

"This fall, I'll let you know. Do you want some desert? I'd like some spumoni ice cream." said Gene.

"I'll have some cheesecake. So co-education certainly improved the band. If they were all guys you wouldn't have been half as interested." said Phil with a twinkle in his eye as he ribbed his friend about his wandering eye.

"You're right. It was the studying of the intensity of the gals along side the guys that drew me in. It seems the gals try harder." Gene replied missing or ignoring Phil's dig.

"This morning Phil, I did my usual. I got up about 5 A.M. and had my strong Peets coffee on the terrace. It was a full moon. For some reason I waved at the moon in a signal of greeting. Here I am at 66 finally getting in touch at a much more intimate level with one of the important influences of my life-the moon. Also there is the sun, stars, fresh air and water. That's where it's at. Everything else pales in comparison. Greater and greater shades of less important influences fill out the rest of my experiences. Those are parts of the essence of life from which we all spring. So my spontaneous salute to the moon surprised and encouraged me that greater peace and sensitivity may be ahead before death. A new dimension showed itself to me. One thing good about death is, I will find out where my relatives and pets went. If you live life correctly, death will be just another event in a rich day." said a whimsical Gene.

"Who do you miss and want to find more?" asked a serious Phil.

"I miss my pets more. We had an unconditional relationship. Relatives are greedy. You can have a great relationship with relatives if you do what they want and talk their language and practice their politics. Otherwise you are just nodded to with or without meaningless conversation and an implied disappointment." immediately answered a dismissive Gene. "That last day could be the start of one great adventure or it may all just go dark. There will be peace. But now you've got me talking violent revolution. Peace and continuity are elusive. Aggravation and discontent are relatively easy to come by. You can give people something to hate or something to love. It would seem that mostly people hate faster. Love comes later when all is explained and sorted out." Gene offers in a bid for a new direction in the conversation.

"I hear you. But first don't get done in by your own government. If you want continuity, get arrested and go to jail. If you want peace you have got to neutralize or get out of the way of war mongers and thieving politicians." cracked Phil.

"Is anything worth going to jail for? Might as well lose your life. Go all the way. Play for the biggest stakes." Gene offered rhetorically.

"How did we get on this topic?" asked a puzzled Phil.

"We were talking about school and co-education popped up. In my mind, girls in the classroom associated with the idea of relationship continuity with women. I think that earlier is better to engage the opposite sex. From that continuity concept came going to jail to achieve continuity and then came choosing to lose your life for an idea rather than be locked up for life." explained a tedious Gene who resented the turn of conversation no matter who turned to it first.

"I'm almost sorry I asked. Your answer over-whelmed my modest question." snapped Phil.

"Actually that was my elevator explanation." explained a recovered Gene.

"For an Empire State Building elevator? Umm... word association? That's a revealing game. Ideas are worth dying for. Animals do it in the wild continu-ally. They do it instinctively. You have to stand for something or else everyone else stands on you. Never rely on some other persons good intentions or sense of justice to make the right decisions for you. That's like believing Congress only acts in our best inter-est." answered Phil with a professors demeanor.

"Speaking of not relying on others. We're sucking in the world with our currency. We print the stuff with no respect to fund the growing socialistic movement here. No socialistic country will ever have a currency that is used as a reserve currency. We will effectively default on our debt by the withering or collapse of the greenback." predicted Gene with assurance.

"Then what country will have the reserve curren-cy?" asks Phil.

"What country's currency will take our place? None look good. We need a worldwide barter system to make sure everyone gets paid what they're worth. With 7 billion humans there can be no free rides." says Gene.

"And no more increase of our population if I had my way." added Phil emphatically.

"I saw a Turner Classic Movie special presenta-tion the other night on one of my favorite actors-Tony Curtis. Robert Osborne interviewed Curtis. He asks good questions and just lets his guests go." said Gene in an effort to lighten up the conversation and to put some new life into it.

"I like Curtis too. Particularly his role in 'The Sweet Smell of Success'-Sidney Falco." said an agree-ing Phil.

Gene picked it back up as if they were in a trivia competition, "'I would hate to take a bite out of you, you're a cookie full of arsenic' says Lancaster as J.J. Hunsecker to Curtis. Curtis should have gone further in his career, but something tells me he wasn't as

bright or as self confident in his own talents as Lancaster or Kirk Douglas. He appeared with Douglas in
'Spartacus'. It's not enough to have talent You have to
know what vehicles are right for you and then pursue
them. There's the so-called breaks also, but brains
make the breaks come your way in the long run. He
did very well in 'Houdini'. He had some comedic roles
but drama was his thing. That face would push open
doors to dramatic leads. Comedy didn't really suit
him. 'Boeing, Boeing' with Jerry Lewis-please spare
me-and 'Operation Petticoat' with Cary Grant really
were dull. They had 'Clockwork Orange' on a couple
nights ago. I'd not seen it in years. Always thought
it one of my favorites. When I saw those unmistake-
able sets I was happy. But I've changed. The movie
is mean and hard. It's still a work of art by Stanley
Kubrick. His use of famous musical numbers from
Gene Kelly doing 'Singin' in the Rain' to Rossini's ' La
Gaza Ladra' and those realistic acting performances
are all very entertaining but the negative intensity
takes a toll. I turned it off. Kubrick's 'Dr. Strangelove'
was dark and tough but done with a tongue in cheek.
Comedy in a dark drama is like having air in a diving
helmet. It makes it fun and endurable."

Phil and Gene notice that Senator Silver gets up
from her table. She says goodbye to the others and
starts to leave. Then she remembers the earlier inci-

dent and looks to their table. She glares at Phil and Gene with the look of revenge on her face. And she wants them to know that something nasty may be coming their way. She leaves the restaurant.

As she leaves Mayor Nuisance gets up and comes over to the table of the two men. The mayor speaks in a mechanical tone. "Hi guys. I'm Gayvin Nuisance. Silver sure gave me an ear full. She doesn't like your politics. Hey, to each his own. I think she said you guys were too liberal?" And then looking at Phil said, "Aren't you Phil Di Caesari?"

Phil answered cordially, "Yes I am. I was a close friend of your uncle Rick. I knew him for over forty years. He was a great guy. This is my friend Gene Ray. But we aren't liberal. How did you know my name?"

The mayor continued to speak in a mechanical fashion. "Someone pointed you out some time ago. It was at a restaurant. I don't remember who did, but I remembered that he said you were a close friend of my late uncle. Anyway, I'm having a rally at the North Beach Cafe this week for my run for governor. It should be a blast. How about you both coming?"

A smiling Phil answered, "Thanks. But I have another engagement."

The mayor looks at Gene, "Can you make it?"

Gene doesn't like Nuisance's attitude. The mayor doesn't listen. Phil told him that they were not liberal. But the mayor didn't pay attention. He's a clockwork. Gene looks up at the Mayor and says, "I'll be honest with you. I don't like your politics. I'm not liberal. I'm a conservative."

It's as if the mayor doesn't hear Gene's response. Because Nuisance launches his pitch in an uncompelling, mechanical monotone. The mayor says "I'm running for governor. I very much share your liberal views. Please hit up my Twitter, Facebook, My Space sites and my own Nuisance For Governor website for details. My message is delivered in seven languages with a sign language link. There's also a nigger-ghetto-projects dialect language link and the Yiddish-speaking dialect link. Part of my website is dedicated to tracking the development of my recently born daughter. There's a mini cam mounted on her head that transmits 24/7. She will be an example of my vision for young Californians. For instance, gay, lesbian, bisexual and transgender nannies will alternate. There are links on my site for people who are interested in meeting folks of the GLBT community.

There are also links for needle exchanges. There's contact info for free legal advice on how to live worry-free in S.F. if you're here illegally. You can download an official San Francisco I.D. We are working on a download for a drivers license exclusive to the City's environs. All are invited to drive in the city. We have car insurance links for second offender illegals and with a get-out-of jail-free bonus card. There's no cash required for insurance. Just pledge that you will pay your premiums when you can afford them. And our team will take care of everything else. Want to be on my team? Deputy mayors salaries start at $98K. Just pledge your first years salary over a 5 year period to my reelection campaign and I will appoint you to head a new bureaucracy of your choice. Illegals are welcome. I have already appointed a gay, illegal Central American to the Board of Supervisors. No problemo. My daughter will take English as a second language in high school. Take a look at the virtual California map that we have come up with. The outdated legal borders have been replaced with the virtual illegal immigration routes that show the true composition of California and where it starts and stops. Hey it's been great kicking it around with you guys. I'm looking forward to seeing you both at my rally. Hey, did you catch 'Milk'? It was a great movie. If you guys are thinking about coming out, we have special advisers standing by. They can help with joint contributions to my campaign while simultaneously notifying your loved ones that you won't be coming home-ever. Adoptions are our specialty. We have links to surgical sex changes and the new chemical sex changes. Want to star in your porn movie? Hey we have directors and actors standing by. Please check out our own version of 'Meals On Wheels'. It's called 'A BLT For A GLBT'. Isn't that G.R.E.A.T.? Bye for now. See you soon."

Phil and Gene look at each other in disbelief. Gene speaks, "He's another screwball Irishman. No matter what the culture or the government, the Irish are against it. I'll bet we hit bottom with this clown. He's polling badly with his nearest rival in San Francisco. I think the whole homosexual political movement is losing momentum. The Halloween turnout at the Castro was way down. The exhibitionism has run its course and they're stuck with more and more disease. Shall we rap it up?"

Before Phil could answer, there was a woman's scream simultaneously with an accelerating car which was quickly followed by what seemed to be a great commotion outside the restaurant. Phil, Gene, Darius and some other diners ran outside to investigate. A quickly gathering crowd blocked the view of Bush Street of what sounded like an accident. Someone in the crowd yelled out that it was Senator Silver who had been hit by a car or it was a near miss. But the car had sped away from the scene. Phil noticed someone he thought he recognized. The other person looked at Phil, smiled briefly and vanished back into the crowd. It was Duesenberg, thought Phil to himself.

"That was Duesenberg." Phil yelled to Gene.

"What do you mean by that?" Gene yelled back.

Meanwhile some police arrived and an ambulance could be heard coming very quickly. By this time traffic had stopped on the very busy Bush Street. People were spilling into the streets. Phil and Gene were immobilized by the crowd surrounding them. They were trying to get information from others close by. It was a kind of basic and ancient information broadcasting based on hearsay and proximity to the scene of the event on top of a time elapse and quality of description ability. It reminded Phil on how quickly modern communication could revert back to another period that was always very close by. Two stories or explanations were circulating in the crowd. Phil heard one explanation that Silver may have been pushed accidentally or deliberately into traffic by a man or woman who's identity or whereabouts is unknown.

Gene heard another story that some car without
license plates pulled away from the curb as Silver
tried to cross the street. Whatever was the cause, the
fact was that Silver was hit and unconscious in the
street.

"I saw Duesenberg. Do you think ...?" Phil couldn't
finish what he was thinking because the crowd shift-
ed and Gene was moved away from a private conversation distance. Was the mild mannered, mid
westerner, a rebellious-take-charge superman just
beneath the surface. Had he just executed an ad
hoc plan of sedition based on a fleeting opportunity?
How many events take place every day that look like
they were the result of long term planning or plot-
ting? But maybe in fact just the result of a recent
conversation yet they set in motion tectonic political
change. Like the Duesenberg conversation with the
two strangers in a restaurant. Was that short talk the
spark for this political rebellious event? The idea of
how chaos lurks so closely when trusts breaks down
is staggering to contemplate. The whole principle of a
democratic civilization is based on the good will of the
people. Without that good will democracy falls apart.
When elected reps become private entrepreneurs and
auction off the governed peoples futures, then all is
fair because then it's a war for survival. There can be
no greater crime than the violation of trust.

"A car without license plates parked at a curb just outside a restaurant where a certain senator is known to frequent at specific periods and specific times could be a grand coincidence when that car strikes that senator. But then add Bill Duesenberg. He mistakes a book title for a call to arms. Then you really have a seminal event. Two people unknown to each other are aiming at a third person for the same reason at exactly the same time and place. That defines convergent evolution. Victor Hugo's 'An idea who's time has come'" said an incredulous Gene.

"It gives me goose bumps" said an electrified Phil. "She was on my short list in the book but someone or others take her out in the real world. 'I could have been somebody.' "Phil said in the same way that Brando said it in 'On The Waterfront'.

"Next you be telling me you 'Love the smell of burning tires and screaming members of congress to paraphrase that line from 'Apocalypse Now'. Phil is this your fantasy of recreating movie scenes or do you really believe in what you plan to do?" asked a somewhat annoyed and confused Gene.

"Shakespeare paraphrased Ovid, the Caesars quoted Homer, the religious freaks quote their respective books because they don't read many other books and everyone has seen the movies. So I quote passages from the movies. There are no new characters, events or new ideas. There are only different names for the ideas, events and characters. You should know that Gene." replied a certain, inspired Phil.

"So where do we go from here?" asked a tired Gene.

"I'm going home. Remember this one thing. We never had this conversation. But keep reading the headlines." instructed Phil who behaved like a person with a new career.

Gene thought. Do I know Phil?

ABOUT THE AUTHOR

Barry Leonardini received his formal education at the Jesuit schools of Saint Ignatius College Preparatory and The University of San Francisco. He was an honor student in classes that included philosophy, Greek and Roman history and language.

Mr. Leonardini was self-employed for 30 years. He traded financial markets from the floor of the Pacific Stock Exchange. He is now retired and lives in San Francisco.

www.ingramcontent.com/pod-product-compliance
Lightning Source LLC
Chambersburg PA
CBHW060619130626
46555CB00002B/569

* 9 7 8 0 9 7 2 8 4 1 6 3 4 *